SEEING RED

T. M. Doran

Seeing Red

A Novel

IGNATIUS PRESS SAN FRANCISCO

Cover art from Adobe Stock Images

Cover design by Pawel Cetlinski

ISBN 978-1-62164-639-6 (PB)
ISBN 978-1-64229-278-7 (eBook)
Library of Congress Control Number 2023944007
Printed in the United States of America ♾

CONTENTS

Part I – Virgil

1. Stars Too Bright 9
2. Starling 17
3. The Circus 19
4. Red Cards 24
5. Façades 29
6. Is the Set Haunted? 40
7. Dire 54
8. Commander Philby 58
9. Last Call 66
10. The Artist 80
11. Offstage 89

Part II – Minerva

12. Scarlet 103
13. The Obsolete Man 111
14. Scorpion of a Script 117
15. Mantle 119
16. The Reptile World 125

17. Revelations (September) 127
18. The Custodian 137
19. Neverland 143
20. Red Card Underground Railroad 150
21. White Cards 161
22. Another Philby 170
23. A Boy's Life 181
24. Pedro 186
25. Grave Matter 197
26. Invasion 205
27. Harbinger 213
28. The Director 215
29. A Girl's Life 221

Part III – David

30. Accolades 229
31. The Philistine 232
32. Windows 242
33. Seeing Red 257

PART I

Virgil

1

Stars Too Bright

June

Out of nowhere, a doe and her fawn darted in front of the car. Castro Hume jammed the brakes with both feet and skidded off the road.

He was lucky this heap of a car hadn't lost a wheel. The Plebeolan was the cheapest rental to be had at the Detroit airport. The vehicle had logged 190,000 miles and felt like it on the 200-mile drive north.

His pulse racing, the screenwriter put the car in park and rolled down the window. He needed a few minutes after that close call. Plenty of people in this part of the country had been badly hurt or killed in car smashes with deer.

So close to the photoplay set, the near-collision couldn't stifle the memories. Five years earlier, Castro had won an Academy Award, and then he succumbed to fame's siren song, giving his wholehearted allegiance to Bacchus. He told himself—at least in the early days—he was smarter than people who couldn't handle success.

As it happened, Castro's tailspin had been precipitous. Since *Stars Too Bright*, he hadn't written a better-than-mediocre screenplay, much less one worthy of Oscar consideration. If producers and directors didn't see Castro as outright poison, they were at least skeptical of him ever recovering his game.

He had been drawn to writing at an early age, beginning

with his fascination with *Shadow Time*, by the way those creative geniuses, Ron Starling and Buck Addison, had combined words, images, and ideas. Starling had been famous in those days as the face of the show. Writers like Addison were practically unknown to most people, just names on the scrolling credits, but not to Castro.

Taking to the road again, he felt a little queasy. Viewing the set once more was bound to crystallize the difference between the Castro Hume of *Stars Too Bright* and the present version.

Scarlet called him an imbecile when he said he was thinking of traveling from Los Angeles to rural Michigan to visit the Trillium set. When he invited her to come along, she laughed at him. He had been an attractive companion when he was basking in *Stars Too Bright* and Academy Award celebrity, and in those days, Scarlet had been happy to hang on his arm. Now, he was on her list of men to call on in an emergency. Whose fault was that? With frequent episodes of drunkenness, Castro hadn't held up his end of the bargain, either.

The Trillium set was immediately visible once Castro had circumnavigated a big hill. Twenty miles west of Harrisville, abutting the Huron State Forest, the set and its surroundings had perfectly captured the setting of the novel, the source material for Castro's screenplay.

Castro entered the phony town on its still-intact macadam Main Street and saw the sign directing visitors to the Repair Shop set, which was in one of the few buildings large enough to accommodate interior scenes. A green truck equipped for off-road excursions was parked outside.

The outer door of the shop was open, as if visitors were expected. Castro pulled open the screen door and walked in.

"Welcome to Trillium," said a friendly voice.

The writer slowly acclimated to the dimly lit interior and focused on the man who had greeted him. He was around six feet tall, clean-shaven, something less than two hundred pounds, with graying shoulder-length hair.

"Jeff Clement," the man said. "You wrote the story?"

When Castro had received permission to visit the set, he had been told that Clement, the caretaker, would be his escort. "I composed the script for the photoplay," he said.

"You're the first person I've met who worked on *Stars*," Clement observed. "All the rest scattered to the four winds and never came back."

While filming, the Repair Shop had been made to look as if it were in use. Now, the dust and dirt were real. "Have they been invited to return?" Castro inquired.

"Only a dozen times, or so I've been told. Harrisville, the county, and even the state sent invitations. No one was interested."

"If the set were in Vegas or L.A., you'd have plenty of visitors."

Clement appeared to bristle at the remark. "Believe it or not, people like it up here."

Good memories aside, there had been days, and especially nights, when Castro had been bored out of his mind on this set. "You're here by yourself?" he asked.

Clement spread his arms. "Yep. All day, every day. I live on site. I do security, tours, maintenance, you name it. We call in contractors sometimes . . . not often."

Castro felt good to be on his feet again after the long flight followed by the long drive from Detroit. He was looking forward to stretching his legs. "You don't mind being alone?"

"I prefer it," Clement resolutely replied. "We have more visitors than you think. A lot of people are still attached to your photoplay."

His photoplay? Castro supposed the photoplay was his, in the sense that the words were his words, at least those lines he hadn't lifted from Lynn Chambers' novel.

"How long you staying in Harrisville?" Clement asked him.

Castro wasn't in a hurry to return to Los Angeles, but how long could a Hollywood writer abide in rural Michigan? This wasn't an active set, after all. "Not long. A few days."

"Let me drive you around the set," Clement said. "I'm always looking for new stories for visitors."

When Alcona County decided to retain the *Stars Too Bright* set as a tourist attraction, the photoplay, like the book, was still enormously popular. But who cared enough now to bother traveling so far off the beaten path? Castro wondered. Even with just one man taking care of the place, the maintenance costs must be substantial. How much longer would the county think it worthwhile to keep this aging set open?

Clement led Castro out of the building, saying, "We still use the well, water tank, and septic they built for the cast and crew; still use the generator to power lights and equipment. All we require is fuel and a little food."

Grasping the truck's door handle, the writer perceived some movement over his left shoulder and maybe a flash of red. He turned his head to look in the direction of where the meadow abutted the woods. "I think I saw someone . . . over there," he said.

"Not likely. You're the only visitor today, and this is government property. That's why the photoplay people were able to build here so inexpensively."

Castro pointed toward the woods. "Someone was moving over there."

"Prob'ly a deer. More deer than people in this county. Get in," Clement said, starting the vehicle.

Castro took the big step into the cab. The inside of Clement's truck was tidy and impersonal, with nary a clue about the man.

Few of the buildings along Main Street consisted of more than a façade and partial sidewalls, just enough for verisimilitude. Prior to filming, the property had been cleared of all but specimen trees. The big oak still stood in the park, along with the gazebo that had been built.

The day they shot Founders Day, Alfred Cooperwasser, the director, and his assistants sat in camp chairs on the far side of the park. All the actors playing members of the Drake family had been present for one of the few all-in scenes. Filming that day had gone without a hitch, and that was saying something with that cast.

No panoptic photoplays for Cooperwasser, a man obsessed with mood, mystery, unexpected turns, and behavior under profound distress. Early on, Castro had learned that every word in the screenplay had to align with that filmmaker's vision for the scene.

Not far from the park was the Drake family home, the largest house in Trillium, where Cooperwasser and his art department had displayed their imaginative wizardry in making a façade and sidewalls plus several miniatures—one of them ten feet by seven feet by three feet—into a convincing chateauesque mansion. The interior sets had been inviting, comfortable, even intimate for a structure with so grand an exterior.

The truck slowly motored past an authentic-looking library with no interior, then the town hall. The water tower was on the next corner, but before they arrived, Clement turned left. This side street, with just a few façades, took them to the train station where the final scene had been filmed. Clement parked the truck, letting Castro take in the station and thirty feet of track on either side of the depot façade.

"I've watched that scene several times," Clement said. "Must have been hundreds of people on the set. How were they all fed and lodged?"

Eyes pinned on the depot, Castro said, "Four hundred eighty-two on the day we filmed Founders Day in the park. Extras were brought in from Harrisville and nearby towns. The food truck was a converted semi with a full kitchen. We rented trailers to lodge some of the actors and crew, and a big top was raised for horses, dogs, cats, the Drake's falcon . . . even the monarchs for Betty's meadow scene. For a while, we had two veterinarians and an entomologist on the set. Somehow, Cooperwasser converted chaos into bravura . . . Am I destroying the magic?" Clement shook his head in lively fashion. "I live and work on an empty set that always needs repairs or fresh paint."

"The sand up and down the tracks reminds me of the sand in our food, in our shoes . . . everywhere," Castro joked.

"In these parts, if sand were gold, we'd all be kings," said Clement. "The glaciers left the sand behind. Drains beautifully, but hard on vegetables."

"You keep a garden?"

"I have enough to do without keeping up with a garden."

Clement returned to Main Street. The stately Drake home, the general store, the town hall, and the park had been the loci of the photoplay so far as the audience was concerned. In fact, only the outdoor scenes and a few scenes in the Drake foyer had been filmed at the fake buildings. Most of the interior scenes had been shot on sound stages inside the big warehouse.

Clement parked across from the gazebo, and the two men stepped out of the truck to look up and down the street. "The buildings are in good shape," Castro observed.

"I paint whenever the weather cooperates and we don't have any visitors. Keeping the same colors makes the job easier."

"The person I saw near the wood line. When we were filming, people would hide in the woods and take pictures of the actors whenever they could get away with it."

The custodian's back stiffened. "I told you no one else is here today."

Castro shrugged. "I'd like to see the interior sets inside the warehouse."

Clement cleared his throat. "Visitors aren't allowed inside."

"Aren't the sets intact?" Castro inquired.

The reply came in a rush. "The warehouse is off limits. We store equipment and tools inside the building. They don't want visitors to get hurt and sue the county."

Clement started for the truck.

"I'll sign a waiver," Castro said to the caretaker's back.

Clement didn't respond until they were both in the cab. "The answer's still no. Might lose my job . . . Get my cigarettes out of the glove box, would you?"

To find the cigarettes, Castro first removed an envelope with Jeff Clement's name written on it.

"Put that back!" Clement bellowed.

Castro tossed the envelope back on top of the cigarettes and slammed the glove box door. More than disappointed, he was furious, but knew that he had better take a deep breath and calm down or he would never see the sets where his best lines had been spoken.

"Can't you make an exception for the screenwriter?" he pleaded.

Clement shook his head, looking straight ahead rather than at Castro.

The writer bit his tongue in the nick of time. "Who can waive the policy?"

"I don't know."

Why should Clement care if he were given permission to enter the warehouse? Castro wondered.

"What else would you like to see, Hume?"

Castro couldn't remember when a relationship had turned so unexpectedly sour, even while working with actors. This trip to the Trillium set was intended to be a restorative experience, but Clement's truculence was unraveling Castro's plans. Sitting in a Harrisville hotel wasn't what he had envisioned when he departed L.A. Scarlet had pegged this trip.

"I'm going to get permission to go inside the warehouse," Castro announced in the tone of voice he would adopt when resisting script changes.

"Go ahead and try," Clement muttered as he parked the truck next to Castro's rental. An awkward silence ensued.

"Thanks for everything." Castro got out and slammed the door.

2

Starling

Twenty-eight years earlier

"What's your name, kid?"

"Castro . . . Hume."

Wearing a gray pullover, jeans, and sandals, a pen in one hand and a cigarette in the other, the man didn't look to Castro half as regal as he did on television, but there was no mistaking those intense eyes.

"Want me to sign the photo?" he asked the boy.

"Would you sign this instead?" Castro inquired, handing the man the script for *Nightmare in the Sky*.

"Where'd you get this?" The man turned the pages. "Transcribed from TV. Buck would throttle the jerk. I'll sign, but don't waste your money on this crap."

"Okay, Mr. Starling. Would you ask Mr. Addison to send me his autograph?"

"Buck doesn't do autographs." The man leaned across the table and looked Castro in the eye. "Why do you want his autograph?"

"I want to be like him."

"Take my word for it, you don't."

"I want to write like him."

"Buck isn't bad when he's on his game."

As Castro turned to exit the line, Starling called out. "Here, send me your address and I'll send you a good script."

Castro grasped the card as if it were a hundred-dollar bill. "Can I have your cigarette?"

The man frowned. "It's a nasty habit. Don't ever start."

"I won't, but can I have it?"

Ron Starling mashed the cigarette in the ashtray and handed it over.

3

The Circus

Castro was still breathing fire when the Plebeolan's instrument panel went dark. The vehicle coasted to a stop with two wheels on the road and two on the gravel shoulder.

He depressed the start button more than once, but the heap wouldn't respond. He slammed the steering wheel with both hands.

Once Castro was convinced the car couldn't be re-started, his anger cooled to despondency. He could call the agency. Someone would have to come from Tawas, at least an hour's drive if they embarked immediately. He could contact a repair shop in Harrisville—how long would that take? He could call Clement and ask the custodian to give him a lift to town, a distasteful idea. Or, he could surmount the tall hill on foot and descend to the Trillium set. As a bonus, this option might secure him a night on the property, something he had hoped for when he left Harrisville that morning.

Castro activated the geo-tracker on his phone and saw that via the hill the route from his current location to the center of the *Stars* set was 1.73 miles; not a walk in the park, but doable. Imagining Clement's face when Castro knocked on the Repair Shop door, he beamed in spite of the inconvenience.

His first impression of Clement had been positive—competent and conscientious, since he was trusted with the property and visitors. A loner considering all the companionless hours. A smoker—Castro had known that before Clement had asked for the pack of cigarettes by the scent of tobacco on the man. But what else besides a craving for nicotine had put the man on edge?

Castro consulted his watch. He would have to commence hiking if he wanted to reach the set by nightfall. He wolfed down the rest of the energy bar and water he had bought at the charging station. He put the car in neutral and pushed it as far off the road as possible without flirting with the drainage ditch. He then locked the vehicle and started walking.

He hadn't gone far before he realized the hill was a giant sand dune, his feet sliding with every step. Castro began to perspire, attracting black flies, reminding him of the hordes of mosquitoes he had encountered during nighttime filming.

He tried to pick up the pace, but that only produced more slipping. Consulting the geo-tracker and waving at flies, he lost his balance and tumbled ten feet down the hill before a red pine halted his descent.

Wedged against the tree, Castro spat sand out of his mouth. No sharp pains, and his head was clear. The phone had been in his hand when he fell. Where was it now? Flat on his back, he turned his head from side to side. Not three steps from where he lay was a skunk, tail raised. Even the maddening flies couldn't provoke him to stir. Heart thumping, Castro closed his eyes, breathing in short gulps, as still as he could be. Any second, he expected to be doused with the animal's spray.

How many minutes of soundless distress passed before he finally opened his eyes and observed the white and black animal ambling down the hill? Frantically, he searched for his phone, finally locating the semi-buried device in a bed of pine needles. Though his clothing was filthy and his elbow rubbed raw, he had avoided injury and being skunked—no small blessings.

The sun was marching toward the horizon. He checked the geo-tracker: 1.42 miles; he had hardly made a dent in the distance he needed to cover.

Trudging up the hill, Castro noted that the flies were back in force. His lungs and legs told him to rest, but on he went, even as the ascent grew steeper. This forty-year-old body, subjected to a dissolute life-style, wasn't well suited for such an adventure.

The first clue that Castro had attained the ridgeline were the blotchy white birch trunks and a refreshing breeze that dried the perspiration on his face and arms.

In the fading light, the forest floor was dappled with light and shadow, birch detritus, and wildflowers like dabs of yellow and red paint. On the side of the hill he had ascended, dotted with lights, was Harrisville, and beyond the town to the east, a massive darkness that had to be Lake Huron. On the opposite side of the hill, directly below where he now stood, was the set, illuminated by streetlamps.

Castro removed his shoes, emptied them of sand, and started down, discovering that descending the sandy incline required a tree limb to maintain his balance.

"One tumble's plenty, thank you," he muttered.

He breathed a sigh of relief at the base of the hill, pitched the walking stick, and followed a dirt path that led to Main Street. He may have been back on level ground, but his hips and calves burned from the ordeal.

Passing the general store façade, Castro observed a woman walking briskly beneath a streetlamp. She had emerged from a side street and now crossed Main a hundred yards ahead of him. What was a person doing on the set at this time of night? When she passed beneath another streetlamp, he observed her straight gray hair beneath a broad-brimmed hat with a red ribbon. Could this be the walker Castro thought he had seen earlier in the day?

She crossed the park and headed for the warehouse, where light was radiating from several side windows. When she reached the building, the woman turned the corner and entered through a door on the south wall.

Now close behind, Castro picked up the pace. When he put a hand on the door handle, he expected to find it locked, but the door opened, revealing a gloomy space. Were those voices he heard? Castro judged that the sounds were coming from the parlor set. Without hesitation, he walked to the double doors and pulled them open.

The parlor looked much as it had when *Stars Too Bright* was filmed: cream-colored walls, rose-print sofa, rocking chair, two straight-backed oak chairs, Papa Drake's upholstered chair, credenza, Persian carpet, piano, and functional gas fireplace. Though Castro knew the piano was just a shell, it looked real enough. Viewers of the photoplay never saw higher than the ten-foot crown molding, and the room had no ceiling, so that booms for sound, lighting, and filming could be lowered into the space.

The set was illuminated by period-piece lamps. On the credenza sat an ivory tray containing cigarettes, the very same tray provided for the principal actors who smoked, and perhaps the same cigarettes as the papers were yellowing.

Who was more surprised, Castro or the occupants, was hard to say.

Seven people occupied the room, four women and three men. Seated on one of the oak chairs was a huge man wearing olive green sweatpants and a short-sleeved shirt. On the other oak chair was a man with a gruesomely disfigured face and hands. Seated on the sofa were two women, one about Castro's age, wearing a sweatshirt that read *Apex Mammalogist*, the other a young woman with trisomy 21; she was slenderer than others Castro had seen with this syndrome. In a wheelchair at the credenza was a thirtyish woman who was missing an eye and a hand. The woman Castro had been following, hat in hand, was standing by the fireplace next to Clement.

The woman with the hat, in her eighties at least, spoke first to Castro. "Looks like you found the circus."

4

Red Cards

"I should've guessed you'd pull a stunt like this," an incandescent Clement hollered at Castro.

"Are you SSB?" the apex mammalogist breathlessly asked.

"He wrote the screenplay," Clement said. "I told you about him."

"You're Castro Hume," the woman in the wheelchair said with emotion.

The screenwriter was so stunned he had forgotten how he looked after the tumble down the hill. "And who are you?"

"I'm Colleen Hardy," the old woman responded.

"For God's sake, keep quiet!" commanded Clement. "Let me do the talking."

"I warned you your storking around the set would get us into trouble," said the obese man to Colleen.

Castro was perplexed. Had these people been cast in a new photoplay? If so, he hadn't heard anything about the project. They were all staring at him.

"My car broke down on the other side of the hill," he said. "I hiked over."

"Of course, after your so-called car problem you chose to hike here," Clement snidely remarked.

"Of necessity . . . May I sit?"

"Suit yourself," Clement retorted. "But don't get comfortable."

Castro sat in Papa Drake's chair. The apex mammalogist

rose from the sofa and turned on the gas fireplace. To Castro, this parlor had always felt so authentic that he found it difficult to believe the constable's lobby was on the other side of the wall.

Old as she was, Colleen sat on the floor next to the fireplace with her back to the police set wall.

The woman in the wheelchair with the missing eye and sock-covered stump of a hand said, "I'm Gina Miller. Were you often here for the filming?"

Castro nodded. "I was here for the duration. Alfred Cooperwasser modifies scripts as he films, so he wanted me at his beck and call."

"I think we should make him leave . . . now," the fat man cut in.

"Don't be silly, Jumbo," the apex mammalogist responded. "He knows about us now."

Rolling several feet in Castro's direction, Gina said, "You must keep our little secret to yourself."

"What makes you think we can trust him?" asked Clement.

"If you don't want me to tell anyone, I won't," Castro answered as if he hadn't heard Clement. "It doesn't matter to me if you live here."

Gina Miller moved even closer. "The truth is, we're all Red Cards."

A panicky sensation came over Castro, brought on by the memory of his sister's fear of receiving a Red Card. Ever since Cynthia's death any mention of Red Cards had caused him to tune out the speaker. Thus, he knew next to nothing about Extraordinary Designation Cards—Red Cards—just enough to know he didn't want one.

"Red Cards are *awarded* to people who are burdens to the state," growled the fat man.

A small, gray, cat-like animal with large eyes, oval ears, and two saber teeth meandered into the room, looking intently at Castro before reclining next to Gina's chair. Castro had never seen such an animal before, but the time wasn't right to ask any questions about it. He was still processing these odd people.

Jumbo went on. "In addition to restricting our employment and medical care, the government insists on knowing our whereabouts at all times. They get upset when Red Cards fall off their surveillance grid."

Castro was aware that services were withheld from Red Cards, but he hadn't known about the surveillance.

"We'll put you in one of the actors' rooms for the night," Clement said. "I'll see to your car first thing tomorrow."

The car was the last thing on Castro's mind. "Where do you get your food?"

"You want to know *all* our secrets?" the mammalogist asked him.

"You don't have to tell me."

The woman displayed a sad expression. "We're at your mercy. I'd climb into your bed tonight if that would protect our secret."

"How many times do I have to tell you this is none of my business?" Castro protested.

"I wonder if you'd take that attitude if the SSB came knocking at your door. Have you ever been interrogated by the Bureau, Mr. Hume?"

To the best of his knowledge, Castro had never met anyone associated with the Social Security Bureau. "Why should they talk to me?" he answered the mammalogist.

She shook her head. "If word got out that you were in contact with AWOL Red Cards and hadn't bothered to inform the SSB, you'd be on their radar."

"You sound like you're trying to persuade him to inform on us, Sarah," Jumbo said to the woman.

"We might as well know whether he's dependable or . . . wobbly," she responded.

Castro knew he was wobbly, but he wasn't going to admit it to strangers. "How do you know the SSB is searching for you?"

Sarah glanced at Clement. "We have it from a good source."

"I'm not a threat," Castro insisted.

"Not a threat!" barked Clement. "Materializing out of nowhere with a story about fond remembrances of this decaying set."

"Come now, Jeff," Colleen pleaded. "If the set's used up, so's the drama. We're a practical lot, you not the least. Let's act like it."

The caretaker frowned but didn't dispute the old woman.

Gina Miller chose that moment to say to Castro, "You asked about food. We have a kitchen garden not far from the set. Jeff hunts game. A nearby lake has plenty of fish. We manage."

"Speak for yourself," the fat man told her. "I've lost thirty pounds."

Castro turned to Clement. "How do you prevent people from discovering these residents? I can't be the only person who's shown up after hours."

"You're the first who came *over* the hill," Clement replied. "We have a motion sensor on the road a mile from here that alarms whenever a vehicle passes. We've had a few close calls when one of us happened to be out of doors—"

"Like the person I saw earlier today?" Castro interrupted.

Colleen quietly raised a hand.

Clement said, "Time to turn in, Hume. Follow me."

It wasn't that late, so Castro could only conclude that Clement wanted to keep him away from the Red Cards.

Before he left the room, Clement addressed the residents. "Make sure you lock the damn doors when you go in or out. How many times do I have to tell you?"

The grim-faced caretaker led Castro down the corridor that had once housed the principal actors' rooms, which had seen their share of boisterous parties, arguments, and trysts in the days when *Stars Too Bright* was being filmed. Clement opened the door to the former quarters of Claude Benson, the actor who had portrayed Stephen Drake, the eldest of the Drake children.

Inside the small room were a single bed, a wardrobe, and a dressing table with mirror and chair. But no ceiling in this room or any other room inside the big warehouse.

This time, Jeff Clement was the one who slammed the door.

5

Façades

Upon waking, Castro immediately knew where he was. Not because he had slept here before—these rooms had been reserved for the director, imageographer, and principal actors —but because he had been dreaming about Trillium, a confused dream in which Cooperwasser and the actors were jumbled up with the current inhabitants of the set.

Before he had fallen asleep, someone had pitched a pair of pajamas over the wall so he didn't have to sleep in his dirty clothes. Small mercies.

Looking up into the high rafters, the writer recalled how underwhelmed he had been when he had seen Brian Bergin's room, no ceiling or private bath. Rooms the five principal actors wouldn't have tolerated in the outbuildings on their Beverly Hills or Malibu estates. The actors could scarcely complain to Cooperwasser, as the director had an identical room. The maestro had shrewdly set Castro up in a pod in a corner of the warehouse, a space not much smaller, and certainly quieter, than the actors' rooms.

Sitting on the bed with his feet on the floor, he heard a loud knock on the door.

Clement didn't wait for Castro to invite him in, pushing the door open and saying, "Your car's in the visitors' lot. When do you plan to leave?"

Castro might not have been the award-winning screenwriter he used to be, but he wasn't going to let the hired help push him around. "I'll let you know," he shot back.

Clement turned on his heels and marched out.

A red and black rug covered half of the concrete floor. The double bed was nothing special. The most elaborate piece of furniture in the room was the mahogany dressing table with a large mirror. Glancing into the looking glass, Castro noticed a modest improvement on the whittled down, sunken-eyed man of six months before.

Dressed in yesterday's clothes, Castro went in search of some food.

A voice behind him said, "There's cereal and fruit in the kitchen." Gina Miller was approaching in her wheelchair. "Want to join me?"

"I won't spoil your breakfast?"

"Not everyone feels the same way as Jeff, but now that you've heard our story you should understand why we have to be careful. With all the excitement, were you able to sleep?"

"By the time I went to bed, I was too tired to think about anything."

She wheeled beside him. "John had your room when he first arrived . . . John Gray is the man with neurofibromatosis."

Castro followed Gina past the parlor where they had met the previous night and the constable's set to the Drake kitchen, not a fully functional kitchen, though equipped with table, chairs, sideboard, and pantry, and plumbed for water and drains.

"I'll make you a bowl of cereal," Gina told him.

"Don't bother. I can do it."

"Let me," she insisted, pointing to a chair.

The woman proved to be adept at getting around, not taking much longer to prepare their breakfasts than he would have required. Movement inside the sock on the wrist with the missing hand suggested she retained portions of fingers.

When Gina wheeled up to the table, Castro asked her how long she had lived here.

"Almost eighteen months. The alternative was terminosapiensis. All of us, except Jeff, are afflicted with things the SSB detests and people fear. You may find this hard to believe, but I'm very happy here."

A few nostalgic days on the set were one thing, but to live in these primitive conditions for months or years was hard for Castro to imagine.

"You're afraid to ask why I look like this," she said, her one eye shining.

Indeed, but he wouldn't admit it.

"I wasn't supposed to be born. The doctor was sloppy with my elimination. My father, the man who raised me, found me and brought me home. I wasn't dead, but as you can see, they made a mess of me. When I survived, the SSB issued me a Red Card and pressed my father to have me terminosapiensized. He resisted, and the Bureau issued *him* a Red Card."

"Was he sick or disabled?"

"In the mind, according to the Bureau."

Though Gina's voice was strong enough, every phrase seemed to sap her a bit.

"Enough about me. I never thought I'd meet anyone so closely connected to *Stars Too Bright*. How well do you know Stephen?"

Another fan eager to see behind the scenes. "You mean the actor . . . Claude Benson."

"He's my favorite," Gina said brightly.

"Did you and your father live near the set?"

"Heavens no . . . a suburb of Boston."

Castro dropped his spoon. "Boston? How did you learn about this place?"

"I'd read a lot about the photoplay and knew where the

set was located, but that's not what you're asking. I'm afraid I can't tell you that."

Gina collected their empty plates and conveyed them to the sink.

"No one knows you're here?" Castro said to her back.

"We don't think anyone knows. That's why we were so worried when you burst in last night."

She spun back around. Castro stood and said, "The government isn't providing any services to Red Cards, so why should they care where you live?"

She gave him a curious look. "You heard what Max said last night. Maximilian Last is our Jumbo. They can do whatever they want to do, and we're defying them."

Defying? This collection of misfits? Might Gina and the rest be mentally ill, in addition to their physical afflictions and conditions? That would explain the corporate paranoia he had witnessed the previous night.

"It would please me if you would stay a few more days," she said, "but don't tell Jeff I said that. Will you walk with me around town?"

Town . . . not the set. This woman's debilitations were many and serious, yet she talked about navigating the Trillium streets as if she were intact and healthy. Gina had said that the man who had saved her paid a steep price. Even if that man hadn't been penalized by the government, why would he have raised such a damaged child—not even his own flesh and blood?

A hummingbird feeder hung from a shepherd's hook adjacent to the warehouse door. One of the tiny birds buzzed Castro as he and Gina passed.

"There's you, Colleen, Maximilian, and John. Who are the others?" he asked.

"The young woman's name is Fiona, and the mammalogist is Sarah. The idomean you saw last night—"

"I'm sorry?" Castro broke in.

"The gray animal. Idomeans are descended from larger African felines that were once bred with another extinct animal. Fiona named him Ghost because he appears and disappears so suddenly."

What was such a creature doing here? Castro wondered.

The woman let Castro push her to Main Street and the avenues of building façades. The library façade evoked a what-else-could-go-wrong scene involving the maverick, Kenny Marks, who had played Oscar Drake, the younger brother, and a local actress—what was her name?—who had gone missing or had walked away before completion of the photoplay.

Gina interrupted Castro's memory. "Those buildings look real in the photoplay."

"Here's something hardly anyone knows," he said. "The imageographer convinced Cooperwasser to change the town's predominant color palette from greens to somber blues. Coop felt green was a natural extension of the countryside. Berkowitz argued that slate and nickel blues foreshadowed the Drake family tragedics."

Gina laughed. "Years later, Jeff stores barrels of slate blue paint in the warehouse for what needs repainting."

The two entered the park on a winding camera pathway. Because one of the gazebo pillars shielded her, Castro didn't see Sarah seated on a bench until he was on the step. At first, the mammalogist's expression suggested that she might stand and leave, but she remained seated.

Gina declined Castro's offer to convey her to a bench, remaining in her chair at the entrance to the gazebo. Maybe she wondered if he was strong enough to lift her.

Castro sat down on a bench facing Sarah, not sure what to say or do next.

"I asked Mr. Hume about Claude Benson," Gina said to Sarah.

Sarah's eyes darted from Gina to Castro. She said, "Gina has a crush on Stephen Drake. By the way, Pasternak's my last name, so now you know enough to get me in trouble if you want to."

"Dr. Pasternak is a renowned professor of mammalogy," said Gina.

Castro happened to glance toward Main Street, where John Gray was coming down the road.

Gina had noticed him, too, shouting, "Join us, Johnny."

Gray started toward them, stopping at a birdhouse mounted on a metal pole and peering inside.

"Johnny made the bluebird houses," Gina said with vigor. "He's an artist."

As John Gray took a seat next to Sarah, a pair of swifts wheeled and shrieked just feet above the grass.

The larger lumps and many smaller nodules on the young man's face were capped with red spots, like little volcanoes. In contrast to Gray's deformities, he had a spectacular mane of long tawny hair.

Gazing about the park, Castro imagined this expansive green teeming with grips, seconds, cameramen, and costumers. When filming was hot and heavy, Cooperwasser had several dozen tradesmen and gardeners putting up things, taking them down, making sure everything was neat, or intentionally unkempt.

"What are you thinking about?" Gina asked him.

"How it was then."

"How was it then?" she prodded him.

Castro had intended to confine himself to a few words about the experience, but the stories kept coming, one after another. No one interrupted him, not even to ask questions.

Gina clapped when he had finished, actually when he had run out of breath.

"What does it cost you to live here?" Castro asked the trio.

The others looked to Gina. "We have no way to earn money. To draw on an account, if any of us had one, would reveal our whereabouts, so the short answer is we don't pay anything. The residents keep the garden, cook, and clean, and we help Jeff however we can."

Gina asked Sarah to assist her to the warehouse. The wheelchair-bound woman looked tired. Castro couldn't imagine how much strength it had taken to do what she had done this morning.

He remained in the gazebo with Gray.

"Don't worry about being nervous at how I look, I'm used to it," Gray said.

The writer was preparing to object when Gray raised a hand. "I can tell the difference between someone who's nervous and someone who's disgusted."

"Gina says you're an artist."

"An enthusiast, anyway," Gray said, looking away. "I have to inspect the garden. I hope we can talk soon, Mr. Hume."

Castro found his travel bag outside the door of his room with the Plebeolan keys on top—for his convenience or to hasten his departure? He supposed that depended on who had put them there.

He wasn't going anywhere. Not just yet. Not unless they made him.

That evening, Gina invited Castro to join the residents in the parlor after dinner. Clement, Max, Gina, and Fiona were already there when he arrived, big Maximilian Last in the same sturdy chair he had occupied the previous night, Fiona sitting cross-legged on the rug, Clement standing by the dormant fireplace, and Gina sitting on the sofa. As her wheelchair wasn't visible, someone must have carried her in. Everyone was dressed as they had been during the day, except Fiona in pink lounging pajamas.

Seeing Castro, the smile on Last's face evaporated. "Hats off, we're in the presence of greatness."

"Yes, Max!" said Fiona, not recognizing the man's cynicism.

Her almond-shaped eyes, upraised at the corners, were bright with excitement that Castro guessed was reserved for idols. What had she been told about him?

"Where did that caravan come from, Jeff?" asked Gina. With the others, Castro had retreated to the warehouse shortly after Gray left the gazebo when the alarm had signaled approaching visitors.

"Iowa," answered Clement. "All seventeen of them."

"Were you expecting them?" Last inquired.

"Not until the alarm sounded. I wish we'd get some advance warning."

"Why should we need to be warned?" Colleen asked upon entering the parlor. "We don't have anything to hide."

"You're home early tonight," Clement chided her.

Colleen turned to Last. "Some have suggested I'm getting old and should behave like it."

Sarah came into the room and sat next to Gina. The last to arrive was John Gray holding a glass of an amber-colored liquid.

Clement said, "John, Sarah, will you help with the fence tomorrow? The deer have knocked down some posts."

Out of nowhere, Last said, "I think Hume should leave tonight. His car's repaired. He isn't one of us. He doesn't belong here. Whether he stays a day or a month, he's no more or less likely to rat us out."

A diatribe, Castro suspected, that had been planned in advance.

"And I say he can leave when he's good and ready," Gina weighed in, surprising Castro with the vigor of her response.

"Me too," Fiona seconded.

Colleen spoke up. "Inviting a person who's done nothing wrong to leave is rude, but considering our situation, I agree it's best for him to move on."

The idomean crept between Castro's legs, leaping onto the sofa and sitting next to Gina. The woman scratched the animal's ear. "Where have you been today, Ghost?"

Sarah glanced at Castro and said, "It's getting late. I say we let Mr. Hume spend another night if he wants to."

Gina said, "I'll prepare snacks. Mind fetching my chair, Castro? Want to help me, Fiona?"

Clement lifted Gina into her wheelchair that Castro retrieved from behind the door. Ghost followed the two women out of the parlor.

Clement waited for Gina to leave the room before saying, "Don't worry, Max. If I say he goes tonight, he goes."

Castro wasn't going to let Clement or Last get under his skin. What did it matter if he left tonight or tomorrow? He had spent a full day on the set. Anyway, weren't these desperate people a distraction from what he had come here for?

Gray and Clement discussed garden repairs until Gina and Fiona returned to the room and set the tray of snacks on the table. "I want you to stay longer, Castro," Gina said. "We can use help in the garden and orchard." Last started to object, but Gina shut him down. "Don't be stubborn, Max. Haven't you learned anything from the misery you've experienced?"

"This isn't personal," Last insisted with a vexed snort. "He isn't one of us."

"One of us?" Sarah joined in. "You sound like the SSB. I thought we wanted to be treated like everyone else."

The idomean darted to the window and launched itself to the sill, attracting everyone's attention.

"Someone's out there," Gina announced.

All of them except Clement converged on the window, the caretaker switching off the parlor lamps before he joined them.

"Whoa!" Gray said with suppressed excitement.

With its nose pressed against the glass was a huge black bear. The animal filled the pane.

"He's cute," Fiona chirped.

"Stand back," Clement whispered. "It's liable to come through the glass."

"That monster's too large to get through," Colleen objected.

Castro retreated several paces from the window while Sarah moved closer. She said, "I wonder if it's a normal bear."

Even as Sarah spoke, the bear backed away and was swallowed up in the darkness. No one moved until Clement turned the lamps on again.

"That's just what we need, one more thing to worry about," Colleen remarked.

His mind racing, Castro excused himself. As soon as the writer reached his room, he recorded the scene with the bear while everything was still fresh. Opening the top dresser drawer to store his journal, Castro discovered that someone had left a yellowed newspaper article inside. Since the set and everything on it had been built less than six years previously, someone must have brought this article here after the photoplay was produced.

"Gianni Grigio's Journey from Art to the Apennines" described how a woodworker had become a sensation in the art world before abandoning his art to join the notorious

Apennine blackshirts. The article had been written decades ago. Why was it on the set?

Castro awoke early. His first inclination was to turn over and try to go back to sleep. Instead, he put on his shoes and went outside in his nightclothes.

It was a still, crisp morning. He hadn't forgotten about the bear, but he wasn't going far and what he planned to do was better done before the others were up and about.

A sliver of rising sun cast a rosy light on the landscape. His writer's eye imagined an omen of blood. Castro quickly laughed it off. He had been here little more than twenty-four hours and was already thinking like those nervy squatters.

He reached Clement's truck without encountering any animals, small or large. Good fortune prevailed when he tried the passenger door and found it unlocked. The writer didn't waste any time, opening the glove box and removing the envelope he had seen on that first day.

By the overhead light, Castro read the letter.

> Dear Jeff, can you accommodate an additional resident? I suspect I'm being watched. That doesn't daunt me so don't let it daunt you, but beware. You can reach me the usual way.
>
> J

Castro hurriedly replaced the letter and returned to his room, unobserved to the best of his knowledge. *Don't let it daunt you, but beware* explained a lot about Jeff Clement.

6

Is the Set Haunted?

During filming, Castro had wondered how comfortable these bedrooms were. After two nights here he had first-hand knowledge: about as comfortable as a third-rate hotel room.

The actors' and directors' rooms were located in a partially finished area of the warehouse—doors, walls, furniture, and lighting.

Nameplates were affixed to each door:

ALFRED COOPERWASSER, DIRECTOR

LOUIS BERKOWITZ, IMAGEOGRAPHER

LETTA LANE, ACTRESS

BRIAN BERGIN, ACTOR

CLAUDE BENSON, ACTOR

KARRIE ZEEB, ACTRESS

KENNY MARKS, ACTOR

How could Castro have guessed that one of these photoplay relics identified a killer?

Before visiting the kitchen, he took a tour of the north side of the warehouse, the area that had once housed film equipment, props, crafts, dressing and makeup rooms, crew lavatories, and his own sleeping pod. The area was mostly open now, housing some yard equipment, paint, a pallet of canned food, and a small work area.

The south side of the building contained all the sets—

library, kitchen, dining room, sitting room, parlor, and constable's office.

Down the middle of the warehouse, from east to west, were the seven reserved bedrooms and reserved lavatories, with corridors on each end for access from the north side to the set end of the building. As wide as those access corridors were, someone had hung lush red portieres to separate the working side of the warehouse from the sets.

On the white wall adjacent to the westerly *portiere* someone had inscribed *S* > *G* in large red letters.

After breakfast, Castro set out for the garden with Sarah, hummingbirds already at the warehouse entrance feeder. Sarah pointed to a red and gold jardiniere overflowing with moss roses on the corner of a step. "That's Gina's garden. You'd be surprised what she does from that wheelchair . . . Was that you snoring last night?"

Castro denied it without much conviction. In adjacent rooms with no ceilings, if someone snored, others were likely to hear.

The morning was clear, though they had been warned to be on guard for a storm.

Castro picked up the box of tools Clement had left outside the door. Except for Gina and Sarah, he hadn't seen anyone else that morning.

"I'll follow you," he said to Sarah, who was already striding north. Soon, the two were passing set façades.

"Who helps Clement with the buildings?"

The briskly moving mammalogist said, "John and I. The others do what they can, but we aren't all suited for ladder work."

Castro didn't think any ladder in the world could support Maximilian Last.

Sarah stopped. "You haven't asked me why I'm here, but

I might as well tell you. I've been diagnosed with terminal cancer."

Castro was stung by her frank words. "Sorry," he lamely responded. "Do you have family?"

"No brothers or sisters. My parents are cosmologists. Their minds roam the universe. Their emotional universes aren't so expansive. By the time I was six we had an unspoken understanding that I'd be an academic success—a scholar in one discipline or another."

"Where did you teach?"

"A university in Maine."

She started walking again. "I was engaged to the provost. My fiancé decided to opt out when he learned about my condition. I had everything—a smart, handsome fiancé, my research, a lovely bungalow five minutes from campus, colleagues I liked and respected . . . everything."

"I'm surprised you gave it up."

"You weren't fooling when you said you didn't know much about Extraordinary Designation Cards. My colleagues learned about the Red Card. You can't keep something like that secret in a close community. They were sympathetic, but my new status changed everything. My fiancé cleared out within a month of the diagnosis. I still saw him on campus, but we did our best to avoid each other.

"I heard about the set from a friend. I was attracted to the idea of getting away for a few days, somewhere quiet and remote. Jeff was walking me to my car when I told him about my condition. He asked me to spend the night in Harrisville and return in the morning. That's when he invited me to stay. I decided to live out my days here rather than settle for a sliver of my old life."

"That's a Clement I haven't met," Castro remarked.

She flashed him a frosty look. "You frighten him, the

threat you represent. When people are frightened, they behave irrationally."

"I promise—"

"Don't," Sarah adjured him. "After my devoted fiancé, I'm done with promises."

Castro recognized the distinctive call of a cardinal and scanned the tree line until he located the bright red bird.

"Can you guess when all this sank in?" she asked. "Go ahead, guess."

He took some little time to answer her. "I suppose when your fiancé left or when you settled in here."

She shook her head and patted her left shoulder. "I knew that everything had changed when they implanted the tracking chip."

They had left the paved street and façades behind and were walking on a dirt path with knee-high grass on either side.

On their right hand was the forest. If the set property was insubstantial, ephemeral, the deliberate art of man, then the forest was the antithesis of the set—one could say its adversary, every timber and shoot and creeping thing programmed for permanence, in its kind if not individual organisms.

Sarah broke into Castro's musings. "Is your family in California?"

Her honesty about her own illness motivated him to open up. "When I was twelve, my parents and sister were killed in a car accident. I would have been with them if they hadn't let me go to a *Shadow Time* convention. One of the happiest days of my life turned into the most terrible."

Castro didn't mention that if he had been with them the accident wouldn't have happened.

"It's hard to tell whether Clement or Last is the more

intent on running me off," he said to move away from the subject of his family.

"Max is complicated. He's smarter than he sounds. You should know that Max repaired your car, not Jeff. He volunteered for the job," she said with a twisted grin.

"How well do you know him?"

"As well as anyone, I suppose," she said, stopping again and peering westward toward the tree line. "Max received his Red Card in his mid-twenties. He was a mechanic in Waco and worked on Colleen's car. She learned about this place and informed Max. They arrived here in a car Max had modified to accommodate his Red Card girth. He can't get under a car anymore but he's a genius at fixing things. I'm not sure this place has done him any good."

"How old is he?"

"Thirty-five."

"He looks older."

"That's the weight. He's not active, and the little he does is taxing, like moving a house."

"What does he do here?"

"Repairs small appliances, tidies up the warehouse . . . He reads several hours a day."

"Last doesn't strike me as a reader," Castro quipped.

"Yet, you think Max is rash because you don't strike him as trustworthy."

Apex mammalogist was more than just sweatshirt bravado.

"Do you think the Bureau is looking for you?" he asked.

"We take precautions. No phones, cars, credit cards, computers . . . devices . . . Nothing having our digital fingerprints is allowed on the set. Jeff has an apartment in Harrisville. That's where he keeps his computer. The only device on this set is Jeff's phone. Of course, visitors bring devices, but they're not traceable to any of us."

"I still don't understand why the Bureau would bother you," Castro said.

"It's their job to bother people like us," she replied with passion. "They get hold of an idea, then they make everything fit the idea."

"There must be more to it than that," Castro insisted.

Sarah shook her head. "A colleague at the university told me there are no incurable cancers anymore, that therapeutic pathways have been mapped out for even the most virulent forms."

"If that's true, why would they let people suffer and die?"

"I asked my colleague that question, and he didn't have an answer, or wasn't willing to answer . . . Why are you really here?"

Castro smiled, but there was no humor behind it. "I was in a rut."

Rut was a tame, not to say wholly inadequate, word to describe all that Castro had survived. He hadn't had a drink in four months. He didn't think anyone knew this. He hadn't even confided in Scarlet.

Not long after Scarlet's rancorous exit, the doyenne of Hollywood tittle-tattle had included this in her monthly roundup of celebrity peccadillos and outrages: "A certain Oscar-winning scribe has lately been seen to be inebriated more often than not. We yet believe he will do the right thing . . . once all other possibilities have been exhausted."

How masterful had that tattler's summation been. All the tragedy, misery, and folly of a life encapsulated in less than fifty words. And how hard that ordeal had been—harder than he had ever imagined. Chills and trembling, heart-thumping and ear-ringing. Desolation.

What had kept him going when he hadn't a soul to comfort or support him? Only the certainty that the thing he loved more than anything else—more than life itself; his writing, his art—was forever lost to him unless he shed his addiction.

He couldn't have managed this trip to Michigan prior to those four wretched months. By the time he had renounced alcohol, all-too-many knew about his addiction and Scarlet had long since uprooted herself from any intimacy with him.

How hard was sobriety now? Hard enough that he still missed drinking and still felt the tug—every day. Nonetheless, he was a different man. He was sure of that much. No one could wage the battle he had waged and come out unchanged. Whether he was a better man remained to be seen.

And whether he could compose anything worthy also remained to be seen.

The problem was, in recent years, Castro's words, expressions, and dialogues had as much life in them as a five-thousand-year-old mummy, and his own life had rudely informed him that the blissful regimen of a happy hour martini, followed by a bottle of Burgundy, with or without some dinner, and a nightcap, wasn't conducive to first-tier screenwriting—not for long anyway. When his happy hours started earlier and earlier in the day, he knew he was in trouble.

"If you're in a rut, you've come to the right place," Sarah conceded. Her smile didn't look any more honest than his had been.

The acre garden had been sectioned off for corn, squash, onions, cucumber, carrots, beans, tomatoes, and melons. Interspersed were patches of herbs; with so few workers, plenty of weeds, too. Surrounding the garden was a four-foot wire fence attached to stout wooden posts. Outside the fence were a dozen mature apple and cherry trees someone had planted long before the photoplay was made.

Castro and Sarah entered the garden through a makeshift gate, passing through stands of early-season corn stalks and melon plants before coming to the east fence, where John Gray, wearing a felt hat with a wide brim, was repairing a breach in the form of a downed post and bowed fence.

The garden was close to the woods, the forest margin bare of color this time of year. Castro recalled the springtime trillium and how it had reminded him then of thousands of bright stars. Closer to the garden fence than the trees were two of Gray's bluebird houses, each with its own design flourish. A small drainage ditch with a wooden water gate at the outlet conveyed excess water away from the lowest point in the garden plot.

"Deer?" Sarah asked Gray.

Without looking up, the man shook his head. "Whatever did this was big and strong."

Immediately, Castro thought of the bear at the window.

"How much damage?" asked Sarah.

"Plenty. Take a look."

Castro set down the tools, grabbed a pair of pliers, and went down on his knees to help Gray remove nails that still attached the fence to the fallen post.

Fiona worked in another corner of the garden. As she strolled from plant to plant, Castro observed her pitching things over the fence.

"She's chuckin' snails," Gray told him. "They do a lot of damage, but Fiona won't let us kill them."

"What if they come back?" Castro asked the man.

"She has a good arm, and snails aren't known for being fast . . . or smart."

The gunning of an engine preceded the arrival of Jeff Clement's truck, lurching and plowing its way through the tall grass between the fence and the woods. Through an open window, the caretaker tossed a cigarette to the ground and hollered, "Have everything you need?"

"Won't take long with Sarah and Hume helping," Gray said.

"Need anything in town?" asked Clement, who had exited the truck and was walking toward them.

"Can't think of anything," answered Gray.

After Clement looked about for a while, he got back into the truck and drove off. Castro pondered what motivated the man. These people didn't have any money. Sheltering six Red Cards was a drop in the bucket of the many thousands who had received that designation. What Clement was doing here wouldn't affect the Bureau's policies, just the opposite. According to Gina and Sarah, they would be obliged to crack down on such offenders. He smiled. Perhaps Clement was nothing more than a rebel with a cause.

Castro helped Gray re-set the post while Sarah joined Fiona. The young man said, "We can use the help this time of year." He whispered, "A lot of work for Jeff and me."

"Sarah looks healthy enough," responded Castro, startled by a lizard that scuttled over his shoe.

"We don't chuck lizards out. They're bug-eaters, along with the bats in those trees," he said, pointing at the forest. "Sarah doesn't complain, but they wouldn't give a Red Card to someone like her for kicks and giggles."

Castro had been around actors for years, even shared a bed with one, and he had learned it was hard to tell what an actor was really thinking. Gray had that protective coloration, too.

"Better pack up," Gray suddenly said. "Weather's on the way."

Castro could hardly believe what he saw when he looked to the west, a dark line of storm clouds, like moving mountains.

"Coming, boys?" asked Sarah, staring skyward.

"Three minutes," Gray grunted as he secured wire to wood.

Castro bore down, too. By the time they closed the gate, the storm was fast approaching.

"Should we run?" Sarah asked, Fiona at her side.

From that turbulent sky came a cold wind. They began to trot as one.

Lightning flashed. Barely a second later, thunderclaps sounded.

Sarah stumbled. Castro clutched her slippery arm, preventing her from tumbling on the path. He felt rain mixed with hail. The wind was bellowing.

Gray was lagging behind. "Keep moving," he shouted.

Rain funneled down Castro's head and into his collar, soaking his back. They endured several minutes of pelting rain and hail before Castro, Sarah, and Fiona reached the warehouse, Gray trailing them by a hundred yards. When the panting artist finally arrived and closed the door behind him, they all looked at each other and started laughing.

"Leapin' Logos," John exclaimed as he barreled into the warehouse. "That was a proper drenching."

Gray had lost his hat along the way. Between breaths, the young man said, "I hope it doesn't damage the new corn."

They could hear the hail drumming on the thinly insulated roof. Sarah, Gray, and Fiona made for their rooms to change their clothes.

Dripping water, Castro opened the door and looked out. The clouds were fraying in the stiff wind, the rain had already slackened, and a strip of pale blue capped the western horizon.

Every stitch of his clothing was soaking wet. Returning to his room, Castro saw that someone had slipped a newspaper article under his door. He recognized Wilson's *New*

York Times review that explained better than anyone else had why *Stars Too Bright* had become such a phenomenon.

> Many have asked how a period piece set in a small town and an anachronistic culture appeals to so many, and the answer is Chambers, and now Cooperwasser and Hume, have created characters with whom their audiences can relate in spades.
>
> Though *Stars Too Bright* is far from high art, it might be considered high folk art. The Drakes live big, love big, hope big, and mourn big. I can't tell you how many have told me they'd trade places with a resident of this fictitious town or that the Drakes feel more real than their own family.
>
> When young Oscar went off to war and died, fans felt as if a beloved brother had died, and when Mabel wandered off and perished in the woods, hearts broke in that mesmeric scene when Jenny Drake embraced her dead daughter. Only Cooperwasser could have wrung such a performance out of Letta Lane.
>
> Through the artistry of Lynn Chambers, Alfred Cooperwasser, Castro Hume, and the principal actors, the Drakes come alive in a big way for millions of readers and viewers.

Castro had little doubt this was Gina's copy of the article and little doubt she had kept it because it described why she was so attached to the book and the photoplay.

The assessment of Lynn Chambers, the author of the novel, always brought a smile to Castro's face: "They told the story twice as well as I'd expected and half as well as I'd hoped."

After dinner, Gina herded everyone except Gray and Colleen into the dining room set rather than the parlor and had them sit at the big table. Gray's absence reminded Castro that the young man had lagged behind the others on the dash from the garden, suggesting the disease had inflicted more than disfigurement.

Five little flames flickered atop the candelabra in the center of the table. Small pewter dishes filled with nuts and chocolates were close at hand, also, a bowl of golden apples. A decorative rug covered the wood floor on this set as in the parlor. Against one wall was a four-legged secretary, above it a painting of nine colorfully attired women, one playing a harp. The other two walls were equipped with false windows displaying outdoor scenes.

"Where are Johnny and Colleen?" Gina asked the group.

From a corner of the room, Fiona said, "John's drinking beer." The young woman then went to the wall cabinet and returned with a small box, placing it on the table.

Castro recognized Alfred Cooperwasser's tune-o-meter. Thousands of tunes were stored on this device. The director had used the music box as a prompt for selecting many film accent pieces.

The girl queued up the Mama and Papa Drake waltz from the anniversary party scene and began dancing with an invisible partner. Struggling to his feet, Maximilian Last joined Fiona, and the two danced the waltz together.

The entire company beamed at Last's whimsy.

Afterward, Last called out, "Everyone knows fat guys make the best dancers . . . Belushi, Gleason, Curly."

Not to be upstaged by Jumbo, Castro said, "Did you know that painting on the wall is an original? It's here because of a wager Cooperwasser lost to Brian Bergin—Papa Drake. That rankled Coop, and Bergin turned the knife at every opportunity, especially when scenes were filmed in this room."

"Papa Drake was so kind and generous," Gina observed, "And such a good father."

Castro couldn't help himself. "Bergin has three children

by three different women, and he isn't much of a father to hear his children tell it. But I'll say this much for the man, he's generous with a bar tab."

The screenwriter prided himself on his glibness, but observing Gina's sad expression, he immediately regretted the remark.

"I'm going after Colleen," Clement loudly announced.

Turning her chair to the false window, Gina said, "Give her a few more minutes."

"Didn't you see that beast last night?" Clement protested. He jumped to his feet and started for the door.

Clement almost ran into Colleen in the doorway. The old woman nudged past him. Before anyone could say a word, she said, "Sorry I'm late."

"You might have said something," Clement responded peevishly.

That wandering nonagenarian had Kenny Marks' old room. For privacy's sake, or as an ironic gesture, she had hung Kenny's hand-lettered *Do Not Enter or Else* placard on the doorknob.

"See any bears?" Last asked Colleen.

"No bears," though the way Colleen said this suggested something was on her mind.

"What *did* you see?" Clement asked.

Everything spelled trouble to this man, reminding Castro of the letter in the truck.

"Probably nothing, or motes in these old eyes. Walking back from the park, I thought I saw something."

"What kind of something?" Clement prodded her.

"Not a bear. Like a shadow with a body attached to it, child-sized, but faster than any kid I've ever seen."

"A fairy," said Fiona. The girl turned to Castro. "Is the set haunted?"

Gina said, "Two sisters from Harrisville who were photoplay extras told Jeff the set was haunted by a witch who killed one of the actresses."

Castro remembered the story, or something like it.

"Where's Johnny?" Colleen asked.

"Fiona says he's keeping company with the beer keg," Last muttered.

But Castro didn't hear Jumbo because his eyes were pinned on the yellow apples on the table. That terrifying memory.

7

Dire

Five years earlier

Castro was stinking drunk. Before and during dinner, he had consumed four glasses of Scotch.

After dessert, Claude Benson, the older Drake brother in Castro's adaptation, stood and dramatically raised his hands. "Who shall bring us a golden apple?"

"Where found, Claude?" asked Bergin, still wearing Papa Drake's white shirt and indigo bowtie.

"In the forest. One of the carpenters said the tree was a few hundred yards into the woods. Who dares?" Benson was no soberer than Castro, and he had an early call the next morning.

"I dare," proclaimed Castro, draining the Scotch and elevating his glass for more.

At the head of the table, Cooperwasser might have been listening. If he was, he didn't join in.

"I dare," said Letta Lane, always good for a larkish escapade, in contrast to her staid character in the photoplay. Though Letta wasn't as young and vivacious as she once was, Castro had seen more than one young actor chatting her up on the set.

"Castro and Letta," Benson said. "An excuse for a tryst?"

Everyone laughed, except Cooperwasser, who said, "I suggest you bring a flashlight, Mr. Hume."

Pretty Karrie Zeeb raised her glass high.

Castro made short work of his freshly poured splash of Scotch, took Letta's hand, and led her out of the dining room set.

The actress grabbed her coat on her way out. She must have been less drunk than Castro because she said, "I hope you know what you're doing. Do you?"

"Certainly, mam'zelle."

She took his arm. With her other hand, she took a sip from a flask inside her coat, then offered it to Castro.

"I don't share my flask with just any man."

Maybe Letta stumbled and was trying to recover her balance but when she leaned into him it was all but an embrace. "Oops, you're strong."

Castro didn't feel strong, as her momentum had backed him up several steps. Cast as the matriarch Jenny Drake, Letta off camera didn't look like the mother of two grown children, or act like it.

Entering the forest, inebriation limited Castro's perceptive powers, but he was aware of the close woodland and night birds rustling and calling overhead.

Twenty steps into the woods—or one-hundred-twenty, neither could have said—the big trees suddenly parted, and they emerged into a clearing. The dark sky was pocked with dozens of bright stars.

"Do you think we'll find those apples? . . . What was that?" she shrieked.

"What was what?"

"That noise. . . . Oh!"

Castro's bleary eyes followed Letta's index finger to three big gray shapes.

Instinctively, Castro lifted the flashlight. "Wolves," he stammered.

"Oh . . . Oh . . . Oh!"

One of the wolves crept to the right, disappearing from Castro's sight.

"Do something," Letta moaned.

The bewildered writer heard a growl to his right. The animal was flanking them while the other two seemed frozen in place. Castro recalled reading that wolves rarely attacked humans, but what if this were one of those rare occasions?

"Do you have anything in your bag?" a panicked Castro asked the star.

"Just these."

Letta produced a cluster of sparklers from the filming of Founders Day.

"Light one," he commanded, praying the chain-smoking Letta had a lighter or match. "Light it, damn it!"

Seconds later, he heard a crackling sound. Castro snatched the sparkler from his companion's hand and thrust it at the flanking wolf.

"Give me another one . . . the lighter, too," he rasped in a voice he never used on the set.

The sparklers blazed. The animals kept their distance. Only one sparkler remained. He dumped the first two sparklers and lit the last one.

"Run," Castro whispered, pulling her along.

The pair scrambled and stumbled out of the forest, not stopping until they reached the warehouse door.

"I've torn my coat," Letta reproached him. "Do you know how much this cost?"

"And nary an apple to show for it," Castro thoughtlessly replied.

Letta wasn't having any persiflage. She stamped a foot. "That's why I hate writers."

Letta had once been the popular child actress Coletta Lane.

In those days, getting whatever she wanted by stamping her foot had served her well. It still worked.

"I'm sorry," Castro said.

"You ought to be. Dragging me into those vile woods. I have to fetch my bag, and you're coming with me." This time, she took *his* hand and led him toward the party room.

Castro could hear Benson's mellifluous baritone before they entered. "Kenny insists she's a receptive dish."

"The local kid, right?" Bergin asked. A smile wreathed his red face. "Did you see Coop when I told him we needed a restorer for that painting? Hah! He couldn't get out of here fast enough."

Taking in Letta and Castro, Benson said, "Ouch . . . I see that the apple was dear bought."

"Shut up, Claude," Letta griped.

"Looks like you could use a drink, dear," Karrie Zeeb pitched in.

Letta sneered at the younger woman, grabbed her bag, and stormed out of the room.

"So, Hume," said Benson, "Let's have that golden apple."

"The wolves guarding the tree wouldn't oblige."

"Hell of a line. Probably a raccoon in heat. So, instead of a golden apple, you return with burred trousers. Rolling about in the heather, were you?"

Castro looked down and saw that both pant legs were covered with burrs the size of grapes.

"Burrs on Letta's back, too, I'll wager," said Karrie to applause from Bergin and Benson.

8

Commander Philby

Castro and Sarah stood in the shadow of the water tower, near the margin of the lawn and the big hill, a paved roadway spur to their right.

"Are you working on any screenplays?" Sarah asked him.

"Nothing substantial. Still clawing my way out of a trough."

Sarah said, "I've been told I'm dying. I can't go back to the work I loved. Now, a day with no bad news makes me happy."

"You said your parents were . . . "

"Dedicated cosmologists first, last, and always."

That first night, could Castro have guessed he would be talking to Sarah about such personal matters? "Did you have close friends when you were a girl?"

"One of my parents' colleagues had three children. I became friends with the daughter my age. Her parents invited me to accompany their family on a two-week holiday." She laughed. "For the first few days, I was confused and anxious, then I began to feel like one of them. They laughed a lot, and when they disagreed about something, they could get loud and passionate. I wasn't used to any of that. By the end of the trip, I'd learned what love feels like.

"They moved west a year later. I've never forgotten them or those two weeks. After that experience, my own family seemed so—I don't know—sterile."

"Are you in touch with your parents?" Castro wondered

if he were asking too many questions, but he was so intrigued he couldn't hold himself back.

Sarah's features hardened. "Occasional messages encouraging me to carry on. I have no computer or phone here, but my cosmologists won't mobilize a search and rescue mission if they don't hear from me. If they fret at all, they'll figure I'm carrying on."

She closed her eyes, turned her head toward the sky, and took a long breath.

The longer Castro resided with the Red Cards, the more their burdens weighed on him: *I've been told I'm dying.*

"Will you be able to see a doctor if you get sicker?"

"Don't you mean *when* I get sicker? Jeff can acquire the painkillers I'll need. He's already squirreling some away."

"What about therapeutics?"

"That's a different story. If medicines can cure me, as my colleague at the university suggested, I wouldn't know where to get them. My Red Card prevents me from legally acquiring any drugs. Terminosapiensis is the SSB's preferred prescription."

"Maybe I can help when I'm back in California."

She shook her head determinedly. "I appreciate the offer, but every connection to the outside is dangerous. Even if I were willing to take the risk, I won't put the others in peril."

From Main Street, Maximilian Last, moving walrus-like in Castro's imagination, called out: "Hume!"

"Must be something important to bring Max across town," Sarah said. "I can't remember the last time he hiked this far."

Breathing hard and sweating profusely, Jumbo beckoned Castro to the gazebo.

Once both men were settled on benches, Last didn't waste any time. "You've been with Sarah a lot," he bellowed.

So, Last had feelings for Sarah. In his mind the intruder

was horning in. Castro tried to compose himself before responding. "I'll be gone in a few days. Gone for good if it's any of your business."

Last shifted, causing the bench to creak. "We take care of each other. I want you to leave Sarah alone."

"If she tells me to leave her alone, I will."

Jumbo's eyes bored into Castro. "So that's how it is. You ought to know—"

Clement's truck pulled up, and through an open window the custodian shouted, "Max, get to the warehouse as fast as you can. A vehicle's on the way—unannounced. Wait, you better get into the truck."

Castro checked his watch—almost four; late for visitors. Sarah must have been alerted because she was moving briskly toward the warehouse.

Clement put the truck in gear and drove over the green to the gazebo, waiting impatiently while Last wedged himself into the passenger seat.

"Do you want me inside the warehouse, too?" Castro asked.

"Your car's in the visitors' lot, so you have an excuse to be here. Maybe it's nothing, but let me do the talking."

Instead of heading back to Main Street, Clement drove diagonally across the park toward the warehouse.

By the time Castro arrived at the visitor center, a black Leviathan had parked in the lot and two men and a woman were emerging from the vehicle. Clement was already there, standing next to his truck.

The taller man was clean-shaven and hard-looking; the smaller man's gaunt face and greyhound physique suggested an athlete.

All three were dressed casually and wore matching black boots. None wore a badge or any other identifying emblem.

The taller man said, "We're with the Social Security Bureau. You're Jefferson Clement."

The custodian nodded.

The residents had said that the SSB were obsessed with keeping Red Cards under their thumbs, and maybe this was proof. This wasn't L.A. or Chicago. The Trillium set was a long way to send three experienced-looking agents for a handful of people who weren't rocking any boats. The way this trio carried themselves, their unannounced presence on the set, and the Leviathan suggested they meant business. The smart thing for Castro was to play ball with them.

Turning to Castro, the same agent asked, "Are you a visitor?"

"That's right."

"You can go," the agent instructed him.

But the woman stepped around the two men and said, "That's Castro Hume, the writer. Hume wrote the script for the photoplay they made on this set."

"How long have you been here?" the greyhound asked Castro.

"A few days."

The woman said, "That's a long time to spend on an empty set."

"My car broke down."

"Did you spend nights in town or here?"

"Why am I getting the third degree?" Castro pushed back.

"Are people living here?" the taller agent asked.

Clement laughed. "Look around. Why would anyone want to live here?"

All three were staring at Castro. "I haven't seen anyone else," he said.

"We're inspecting the site," the taller agent announced. He pointed at the warehouse. "What's inside?"

Clement shrugged. "Yard equipment. Interior sets. Actors' still furnished quarters. I live there."

"Alone?" the woman asked.

"So far."

How would Clement explain his lie when the SSB agents entered the warehouse and discovered the Red Cards? Castro wondered.

The taller agent looked in the direction of the building. "Your food purchases are more than one person's needs."

"That's all? I'm a big eater, and I feed the animals."

The agent kept at him. "How many entrances to this building?"

"Two, but I keep the one on the other side locked. Kids come over from town sometimes. I don't want them sneaking in."

"We'll walk the site first, then meet you at the warehouse door, Commander Philby," the taller agent told the woman. "Let's go," he said to Clement.

So, this Philby woman was running the show, and by leaving her here they were making sure AWOL Red Cards didn't sneak out while they were inspecting the set. Castro made as if to follow the men.

"Stay," Commander Philby ordered him. Once the site manager and the agents were out of earshot, she said, "We know he's up to no good, and it needn't involve you."

Her eyes shifted to the woods behind the building. Castro recalled something a make-up artist had told him: that he preferred to work on nondescript faces rather than beautiful or distinctive faces because a blank canvas was more receptive to his art than one already busy with detail. Looking at Philby, Castro understood what that make-up man had meant. The blank canvas of her face could be made into anything.

"Your photoplay wasn't bad for a melodrama," she said. "You won an Oscar, didn't you?"

Castro flinched inside. "They give Oscars for melodramas, too. They look the same as Oscars for artistic films," he said.

Her expression never changed. "How long were you on this set?"

"About ten months."

The woman pointed to the tree line. "Mabel got lost in those woods."

Mabel Drake, a character in *Stars Too Bright*, had wandered away from home, gotten lost in the woods, and died from exposure—the dramatic scene Wilson had identified in his review of the photoplay. Why had the commander mentioned Mabel?

"Ever heard of Gianni Grigio?" Philby asked.

"No, should I have?"

"Grigio had a son. We'd like to know where he is."

"Sorry, I can't help you."

"Sometimes, people answer without thinking about the consequences."

She knew, or suspected, he was lying. This was his chance to set the record straight. Maybe that was why the other two agents had removed Clement from the scene, so Philby could interrogate him without his being influenced by the custodian.

Castro didn't take the bait. He pointed to Clement's truck and said, "I need a cigarette from the glove box."

Philby surveyed him from head to toe and glanced again at the woods. "Hurry up," she said with a scowl.

Castro came back with a lit cigarette, took several furious puffs, and tossed it to the pavement.

"Where have you been spending your nights?" Philby asked.

"Inside the warehouse, in an actor's room."

"If anyone else was living here, you couldn't have missed him." She was giving him the look a director gives a problem actor. "You haven't done much lately, have you?" she added.

As Castro was about to answer, the two male agents and Clement approached. "You missed an opportunity," Philby said to Castro. "You won't get a second chance."

"And you've done your duty. Don't worry about mine."

Philby made a disparaging sound, turned, and said to Clement, "We're ready to go inside."

The custodian led the three agents into the warehouse. Surely, the SSB would find things in the rooms that weren't photoplay artifacts. Castro's mind was racing, as it did when he was reimagining scenes. Could he use the excuse that the squatters had remained hidden while he was on the set?

When Clement and the agents returned, Castro expected them to be accompanied by Sarah and the other Red Cards, but no one else emerged from the building. How had six adults, none of them agile—one weighing over four hundred pounds and another in a wheelchair—concealed themselves? And why weren't the agents carrying bags of evidence?

"Have you checked the truck?" asked Philby. "Then do it."

A look of alarm froze Clement's face.

The lean agent spent a few minutes inside the truck, then returned shaking his head.

Philby looked from Clement to Castro. "We're leaving, but we're not finished here. If people are living illegally on these grounds, we'll find them, I assure you." She stared hard at Castro. "You don't need any more trouble, Hume."

The agents piled into the big caravan and sped off.

Watching the car, Clement said, "I think she likes me."

But Castro had been around actors a long time, and Clement couldn't carry the scene. The custodian was scared.

9

Last Call

Clement appeared at the door of Castro's room. "We're meeting in the parlor."

After the custodian left, Castro sat on the bed and put his head in his hands. Should he attend the meeting and risk being pulled in even deeper, or should he get the hell out of here? Leaving made the most sense, but he felt compelled to hear what Clement and the residents had to say about their vanishing act.

After Philby and her cohort left the set, Castro had kept an eye on the wood line, expecting the Red Cards to emerge at any minute. How surprised he had been when he had entered the warehouse and found them there.

Everyone except big Last was present when Castro arrived in the parlor. Colleen was speaking to Clement. "I haven't seen him since we . . . since those people left."

They all looked shaken, even the reliably composed Gina.

Clement strode purposefully out of the parlor.

"Has anyone checked Max's room?" Gray asked.

"I did," Sarah replied. "His travel bag's gone."

"Where did you go when they searched the building?" Castro asked them.

"We aren't supposed to talk about it," Colleen said.

Castro knew the building had no attic or basement. Had the residents escaped through the rear door and used the warehouse to shield their flight into the woods? He supposed it was possible, though from where he and Philby had been standing, that escape route would have been an extremely narrow corridor. And how could Gina and Last have managed such a hasty retreat?

Exasperated, Castro said, "Aren't you allowed to think for yourselves?"

"Apparently, Max has no difficulty thinking for himself. He's gone . . . with my truck," Clement said from behind Castro.

"No!" someone moaned.

"I see no other explanation. Max and my truck are gone."

"Why would he do such a thing?" Colleen asked, emotion in her voice.

"The SSB spooked him," suggested Gray.

"He must have known this would put all of us at risk," Gina said. "That doesn't sound like Max."

Sarah spoke up. "I'm responsible. After we . . . after the SSB left the site, Max took me aside and told me how he felt about me." She looked down at the floor. "I didn't give him any encouragement."

Had Castro's encounter with Last in the park sparked all this?

"Then I'm afraid the game's up," Clement said. "Max can't lose himself in a crowd. If the SSB talked to the police, Max will be arrested and so will the rest of us. If you can find a way out of here, I advise taking it."

"Wait a minute," Castro protested. "Last can't have gone far. Even if he intends to bolt, he'll have to stop in Harrisville to provision himself. Clement and I can go into town in my car and try to find him."

"Then what?" Gray demanded. "You can't carry him back."

"Hopefully, you find him before the police," Gina said.

Clement didn't resist Castro's suggestion, and the two men didn't waste any time making for the lot.

Once they were on the road to town, Castro pushed the Plebeolan. "Have you had SSB agents on the set before?" he asked the custodian.

"Never," Clement responded. "You heard me mention the furnishings in the actors' rooms. I didn't count on one of our birds flying the coop."

"The condor."

Clement did him one better. "And two parakeets have to bring that condor back. I sure as hell wish I had a cigarette. I don't smoke inside the warehouse because of Gina—her condition. What did the SSB woman ask you?"

"Commander Philby . . . she asked me about a man named Gianni Grigio. I found an article about Grigio in my dresser drawer. Philby said they're looking for his son."

"I never heard of the man," Clement remarked.

"Gianni Grigio is the Italian version of John Gray."

Clement cleared his throat nervously. "I have to ask you something. We've been unmolested for almost two years. You arrived a few days ago, learned all our secrets, now the SSB raid the set. That's not a good look."

Castro bit his tongue. This was no time for another tussle with the site manager. "I didn't tell them. I haven't communicated with anyone since I've been here."

"Let's say you're telling the truth—"

"I am, the whole truth."

"Then it's a coincidence Philby showed up, or else they were tailing you."

Why would the SSB be following him? He had no idea what was going on here when he left California.

"Or . . ." Clement cut into the writer's thoughts, "they

had some evidence that put the set on their radar and your coming here tipped the scales."

"Maybe the evidence they had triggered satellite surveillance."

"That's not what happened," Clement curtly returned. "All right, you know enough to bury us, so I might as well tell you the rest. The satellite images for this site are modified."

Castro was so immersed in this conversation that he had to admonish himself to focus on the winding road lined with deer-infested woods. He began thinking out loud. "Something drew the Bureau's attention to this site. Then I came here, prompting the raid. But they didn't find anything. At least, we don't think so. If they fix the corrupted site images—"

"I can't worry about that," Clement insisted. "True images are bound to betray us. The residents can't remain indoors twenty-four seven. Every day of freedom is a victory. Yes, a victory."

Was Clement trying to convince Castro or himself?

On the outskirts of Harrisville, Clement pointed to a log cabin on a gravel lot.

The caretaker's green truck was parked out front. Castro pulled in next to it. Only a handful of trucks and cars were in the lot, none of them Philby's Leviathan.

Before they went inside, Castro reached into his back pocket and produced the folded envelope that had been in Clement's glove box.

The custodian's eyes widened. "I was sure the SSB found it. How . . . ?"

"I told Philby I needed a cigarette from your truck, then I stashed the envelope."

"The devil you did!" Clement exclaimed. "You took a hell of a risk."

Castro handed the envelope to Clement. This wasn't the time to reveal he had read the letter or to ask any questions about the identity of J.

The rustic bar had a plank floor, dim overhead lights, and a dozen patrons, half of them card players, all of them over fifty. Last was sitting alone on two side-by-side chairs at a table in the corner with a glass of beer and a basket of chips on the tabletop. His blue button-down shirt and brown slacks were the smartest clothes Castro had seen on the man.

Their quarry looked up at Castro and Clement as they approached the table. "I see you've found me," he said to Clement as if Castro weren't present. He was already drunk, though not yet stupid drunk.

"Let's go, Jumbo," Clement said softly.

"My name is Maximilian," the man growled.

"Have it your own way, Max. Let's go."

Many of the patrons were watching them, sensing, as barflies do, that something was up.

"I'm not going back," Last muttered through clenched teeth.

"Don't be stupid."

"I'm not stupid, I'm fat!"

"You're smart enough to know you're putting the others in danger."

"I figured if I could get out of here fast, I wouldn't cause trouble for the rest of you."

Before he could check himself, Castro said, "Getting drunk in public is getting out of here fast?"

Last's nostrils flared, though he seemed committed to Castro's invisibility. "I wasn't going to steal your truck, Jeff. I planned to leave it in Harrisville and take the bus to Detroit."

"Let's put all our cards on the table, Max. Sarah told us about your conversation."

In spite of the beer's dousing effect, Last's eyes kindled like stoked embers. "It's a settled order of nature that women prefer Oscar winners to trolls," he said. The glare he gave Castro added, *I told you I wasn't stupid.*

The big man drained his beer glass and shoved a handful of chips into his mouth, spraying crumbs far and wide.

"A few days until this business blows over," Clement pleaded in a soft voice.

Last swept the bag off the table, clambered to his feet, and anchored himself like a heavyweight boxer preparing to take a punch. Clement started walking toward the door.

The bartender shouted, "He owes me seventeen-fifty."

The custodian tossed a twenty on the bar.

The three men walked outside into a setting sun. At the truck passenger door, Last moaned and clutched his chest.

"Shit!" Clement exclaimed. "Hold him up."

The big man slid down the side of the truck. Try as they might, Castro and Clement could only slow the man's descent to the ground.

Last was as still as death. Finally, he shuddered and spit on the gravel.

"What's wrong, Max?" Clement asked anxiously.

In a fugue state, Last managed to sit with his back against the truck. "Dizzy . . . pressure," he murmured.

"I'll call for help," Clement said.

Bathed in sweat, Last shook his head resolutely. "Don't you dare. Bring the SSB like flies. Give me a minute."

They waited, Castro fretting that someone would exit the

bar and witness the scene. Even though it wasn't yet dark, lights came on around the name on the building: Last Call Cabin.

"Take me home," Last gasped, as he got to his knees. His shirt and pants were a mess.

"Are you sure?" Clement asked.

"I'd rather die here or on the road than have the SSB find me. Help me up."

Castro and Clement helped steady Last, but only the man himself could do the heavy lifting. With the passenger seat all the way back, Last squeezed inside, his chin pinned to his chest, sweat streaming down his face.

Clement hurried to the driver's seat. Castro followed them out of the lot in the rental car.

What had he gotten himself into?

Gina, Sarah, Fiona, and Colleen were waiting outside the warehouse door. When Last didn't get out of the vehicle, Colleen asked, "What's wrong? What happened?"

No sooner had Clement stepped out of the truck than he lit a cigarette and took a long draw. "We found him at the Last Call. On the way to the truck, he had a fit."

"What kind of a fit?" demanded Sarah.

"The kind where you lose consciousness."

"It's probably his heart, Jeff. How did you get him into the truck?"

This was the residents' show, so Castro kept his distance.

"Max came to."

"Is he conscious?"

"Just a few words on the way back," replied Clement.

"People in the bar must have seen him," Colleen observed. "Not good."

"Let's see if we can get him inside," Clement suggested,

opening the passenger door slowly to make sure Last didn't tumble out.

"Are you awake, Max?"

"Yah."

"Can you get out?"

The man nodded.

"We'll help," Clement said.

Last emitted a hoarse laugh. "Think you're up to it?"

"Here, Jumbo," Fiona said, handing the big man two canes.

Castro and Clement each supporting an arm, Last shuffled inside and to his room where they helped him undress and put him to bed.

Following them in her wheelchair, Gina said, "Give him these two aspirins. If it's his heart, they may help."

Sarah persuaded Last to take the medicine, after which he closed his eyes.

"I'll check on you in a while," Sarah said.

Gina wheeled to the head of the bed.

"Max!" Gina called out.

The prostrate man opened his eyes. His face was deathly pale.

Gina held a miniature glass flask in her intact hand. She removed the stopper. "May I anoint you with this oil, Max?"

Last blinked several times.

Gina must have taken this for concurrence because she used her damaged hand to pour a generous amount of oil into the palm of her intact hand, smearing it on the big man's forehead. Within seconds, the room was suffused with a sweet fragrance.

The others, intentionally or through an unspoken sympathy, had formed a half-circle around the wheelchair.

"Peace, dear friend," said Gina.

Last closed his eyes again. His panting subsided.

The woman in the wheelchair delayed a minute before leading them out of the room.

All the others followed her to the parlor. The custodian grabbed a cigarette from the ivory tray on the credenza.

A single lamp illuminated the space, and that on a low setting. Even though Last and Gray were absent, the room felt small to Castro.

"Go ahead and smoke," Gina said.

But Clement returned the cigarette to the tray.

"What a day," observed Colleen. "I'm exhausted."

"We have to talk," Clement said. "Did you see or hear anything after we left the set?"

The residents shook their heads.

"That doesn't mean those agents aren't skulking around," Castro observed.

Gina joined in. "Could the tracking chips have led those people here, Jeff?"

"I told you, you don't have to worry about the chips," Clement responded, casting a furtive glance at Castro.

"Perhaps you told us that to make us feel better," Sarah protested. "Those chips were implanted for a reason."

"Where's John?" Clement abruptly asked.

No one answered him.

"Fiona, check his room," the custodian ordered.

Fiona marched out of the parlor like an army private on a drill field.

"Try to be kinder to her," Gina admonished Clement. "She's a *person*, not a dog."

Colleen gave Gina a harsh look that vanished as suddenly as it appeared, a look Castro never expected to see on the old woman's face.

"Shouldn't we find a doctor for Max?" Sarah asked everyone.

"He doesn't want one," Castro said.

"He needs a doctor whether he wants one or not," Sarah insisted.

"We can decide tomorrow," Clement said.

"If he's alive," Sarah returned. "I feel responsible."

"Forget about that!" Clement barked. "He's the one who caused this ruckus. Now, we'll all have to be more careful when we're outdoors—"

"Sorry, Jeff," Sarah interrupted. "If the SSB suspect something, how careful we are doesn't matter. They'll find us."

Fiona was inching into the room. Clement noticed her and softly said, "Fiona, I'm sorry for speaking to you that way."

Fiona's face brightened. "John's door was locked."

"Where did you go when the SSB were here?" Castro asked them again.

"If you don't know, you don't have to lie," Gina answered him.

Gina's gentle response wasn't enough for Sarah. "You've seen us dashing about like mad creatures. Isn't that enough for you?"

"At least tell me why they didn't learn that you're living in those rooms."

The Red Cards looked to Clement.

"The residents aren't allowed to keep photographs or anything bearing their name on the set. Also, they have personal bags they conveyed with them when the SSB were here. We're careful, Hume."

Sarah said, "Jeff, you need to know something about being careful. Max used the computer you brought to the set last month. He knows I don't have access to scholarly articles, so he found some he thought would interest me. That could have alerted the Bureau. I told him to stop, but I may have been too late."

The site manager scowled and made fists with both hands. "What next?" he said.

"Has anyone ever left the set before this?" Castro inquired.

"Why would you ask that?" Clement fired back. "Or are you trying to . . ."

"Go ahead and finish. Am I trying to pin the blame on someone else for the SSB coming here?"

"John went off, didn't he?" Fiona said with a grin.

"That's enough, Fi," Colleen snapped.

An emotional frost seemed to descend on everyone except Castro. He looked around the room. No one would meet his eyes, not even Gina.

"Six months ago . . . just one night," Clement said.

"Where was he?"

"How the hell should I know?"

"Gray didn't say anything?"

"Haven't we had enough for one day, Hume? No one's jumping on you."

But Castro persisted, more curious than concerned. "Just answer one question. Did he take your truck as Last did?"

"No, he didn't *borrow* my truck."

"Where did he go?"

"That's two questions."

Though Castro's inner voice told him he had said enough—perhaps more than enough—he was in a heady mood. "Gray couldn't have hiked to Harrisville."

Colleen cleared her throat, and said, "Here it is, Castro. No, don't stop me, Jeff! Johnny is twenty-seven—a young and lonely man. He found a way into town. Jeff had been warning us for a week that a big bus was coming to the set—enough visitors for John to lose himself in the crowd when they departed. Tour buses stop in Harrisville for fuel, snacks, public lavatories, before heading for the highway. John could have spent the night in town and hired a car the next day to drop him off near the set. Easy to come out of the forest as if he had gone for a walk or to the lake."

Still, no one was sitting, except for Gina in her wheelchair.

"A cold December day. John wore a coat, gloves, and his father's hat. He had admitted to several of us that before he came to the set he had often used makeup on his face. On a December afternoon and evening, he might pass for ordinary.

"We think he paid for amorous companionship." Colleen clipped on briskly, as if the artist had purchased a hamburger.

"When Johnny returned, he was more distant than usual. We didn't speak of it. We pretended that night never happened. But he knew we knew he'd been up to something."

"A few days later, I found the makeup kit in the trash," Clement added. "Maybe John wanted me to find it, to let me know he wouldn't do it again."

"Maybe," Colleen muttered.

Ghost crossed the parlor and hopped onto Gina's lap. One by one, Clement and the residents left the parlor, until only Castro and Gina remained.

The image of Gina, Last, and the oil was still vivid; the fragrance, and how her act had temporarily buoyed the others.

Scratching the idomean's crown, Gina said, "Do you know what I most admire about your story?"

"Lynn Chambers' story," he automatically corrected her.

"*Your* story, Castro. The novel depicted misery—Mabel's and Oscar's deaths—but the story wasn't about unremitting misery. It had love, friendship, and hope, too. You stayed true to what made the story so admirable."

If he had done that, it had been unconscious, or to sustain a dramatic arc, or to accommodate Cooperwasser, whose vision drove the photoplay, but hearing that his screenplay had pleased Gina made him happy.

"May I wheel you to your room?" he asked her.

"Ghost may not like that. He's satisfied with the status quo. He's a gen-alt, you know."

Not for the first time, Gina had surprised him. "I thought gen-alts were confined to research labs and high security preserves. How did you ever get one?"

She gazed down at the animal. "Ghost doesn't belong to me. He chose to join us, and he chooses to stay."

"You're a courageous woman," Castro said.

Gina smiled at him. "One must face things as they are. Listen to me, Castro. Those people will persecute you if you're here when they find us. That would make me very sad. Now, I will accept your offer of conveyance, Sir Galahad."

Fiona was standing outside Gina's open door. Gina didn't seem surprised to see the young woman there. No words were spoken.

Castro left Gina and walked down the silent corridor to his own room. After all the time he had spent in this building, why should he still be surprised when he looked up and saw the warehouse rafters?

He remembered the time a small bird had found its way into the warehouse and Karrie Zeeb had gone on a rampage until it was killed and disposed of. When she had complained on the set, Kenny Marks, who portrayed the heroic younger brother, Oscar Drake, in the photoplay, cynically said, "I shall scale the rafters and stalk the vile creature with Mabel's butterfly net. Anything for the great Karidiana Zeeb." Kenny could be humorous and cutting at the same time. You didn't want to be on the cutting side of that actor's humor.

Castro hadn't seen any birds inside the warehouse this time, but mice had been another Karrie obsession, and he had seen a few in the warehouse storage area.

It was after midnight. He was tired, confused, angry, and frightened. If that weren't bad enough, he had cut a finger on his door handle, requiring a sticky bandage from his travel bag.

Castro was undressing when the idomean sauntered into the room. The mice around here had better be on guard, thought Castro. "Make yourself comfortable," he said to Ghost.

10

The Artist

Opening his eyes the next morning, Castro saw a blurry Ghost sitting upright on the dresser. The writer had left his door cracked so the animal could leave the room. If the idomean had gone out during the night, it had decided to return.

Ghost followed Castro out of the room, but the animal went in the opposite direction when Castro made for the kitchen. Castro ate a bowl of cereal and some early berries. A handwritten note on the table, authored by Clement, told him that John, Fiona, and he had gone to work in the garden.

The events of the last few days—his discovery of the Red Cards, the SSB raid, Max's flight to Harrisville—had fogged Castro's mind and emotions. He couldn't imagine where the Red Cards had hidden when Philby and her men scoured the site.

The sun was shining, lifting his spirits as he walked north from the warehouse. "No damage today?" Castro asked Clement at the garden fence.

Clement shook his head without looking up from his hoeing. Fiona was weeding, and Gray was shoring up the fence.

"How can I help?"

Clement lifted his head. "John could use a hand with the fence. Brackets and wire are in the corner."

Castro found an anchoring post that required reinforcement. Putting on gloves, he went to work.

When Clement announced that he was going to the forest lake to fish, Fiona jumped and clapped.

The remaining three kept working. Castro lost himself in the manual labor, first fence repair, then weeding.

Gray broke a long silent spell. "Let's pack up. You finished?" he asked Castro.

"I'm ready," the writer responded. "Gardening is hard work."

"Invaders great and small, and the elements—nature's art," Gray responded.

"You call that art?"

"I'm nature's art, too," Gray proclaimed with a mischievous grin.

If the idomean was a mystery, John Gray was a bigger one. How could it be a coincidence that Castro had found an article here about Gianni Grigio, a famous artist with the Italian version of the name John Gray?

Heading back, Gray said to Castro, "Gina told us Letta Lane drowned in the ocean."

Castro hadn't been close to Letta, but he hated thinking about her end. "Off Malibu. A few days before a cast and crew reunion. Letta's death put a damper on the celebration."

"What happened?" Gray asked. "Gina didn't know much about it."

"Party on the boat and rough water."

"Was she murdered?" Fiona loudly asked.

"Letta wasn't a good swimmer." Castro didn't think the actress' drinking needed mentioning. If he and Letta had been on a boat that night in the woods, both of them would have fallen out.

Gina was waiting for them at the warehouse door. "Where is Jeff?" the woman nervously asked.

"Fishing," returned a joyful Fiona.

Castro said, "I'm surprised any fish are left in the lake with that big bear around."

"Jeff's as good a fisherman as that bear," insisted Gina.

Castro wasn't convinced, especially if the two were fishing at the same time. "I'd like to see that beast in broad daylight."

Fiona gave Castro a wide smile. "Me, too."

"If you think that bear is scary," interrupted Gray, "you should have seen the *ba-hee-muth*. Fi saw it, too."

"Mammoth," Fiona delightedly added.

"Here?" Castro asked in amazement.

Gray nodded enthusiastically. "Last fall. Came out of the forest and crossed the meadow."

While in Michigan for the photoplay, Castro had learned about the herd in the northern peninsula, but no one had suggested mammoths had ever come this far south.

Castro excused himself, retrieved his journal, and made for the parlor. He hadn't been working long when Fiona approached him, put a finger to her lips and motioned for him to follow her.

Around the corner was the constable's set. Fiona looked both ways, opened the door and led him in, then closed the door behind them.

Unselfconsciously, Fiona took his hand and, with a little pirouette, led him behind the Trillium constable's desk to a wooden platform supporting stainless steel tanks. In a back corner sat a washer, dryer, and a small tub.

"Beer," she whispered in his ear.

"Who's in charge?"

"Jeff and John." Fiona made a sour face. "Do you like beer?"

"Too much," he admitted.

"John likes beer too much, too. I want you to stay," she solemnly added.

"I can't stay. When I leave, you'll be safer."

Fiona's face fell. "When are you going?"

"Soon."

"Can I come with you?"

One surprise after another with this young woman. The idea that anyone would trust him this much scared him. Castro shook his head. "After a few days with me, you'd be ready to come home."

Fiona lowered her eyes. "Someday, I want to marry. How do you do that?"

He wasn't expecting that question, either. Unlike the rest, Fiona didn't see her Red Card as a life sentence.

What should he say that wouldn't discourage his new friend or make waves for the rest?

"I'm no expert," he began. "People have told me it's best to start as friends."

She looked up at him. "I had a friend in Boston. His name was Jimmy. He was funny. They took him away. I wish I could find him."

Her words struck Castro to the heart. Expressed in countless ways, wasn't this one of life's most profound desires? *I wish I could find him . . .* or her.

"They told me he went to California. Why didn't Jimmy say goodbye?"

Of course, they would have told Fiona that, and the reason she wanted to come with him—to find Jimmy.

His anger smoldered, but what purpose would be served

by allowing it to blaze? He might as well be King Canute attempting to hold back the sea for all the good his anger would do.

"John told me the train goes from Detroit to California. I rode a train with sixty-seven chickens . . . thirteen rabbits . . . three pigs."

Castro smiled at Fiona's inventiveness.

He accompanied her back into the open area of the warehouse, expecting to part company with her. Instead, Fiona took Castro by the hand and led him to her room.

The inside was much like Castro's room and that of the others because Cooperwasser had been careful to ensure that the actors' facilities were exactly the same size and equipped with identical furniture. What distinguished Fiona's room, though, were the many items displayed on top of her dresser.

Fiona picked up a painted wood carving of a goldfinch and handed it to him.

"This is beautiful," he said, imagining Fiona carefully placing each of these treasures inside her personal bag when the SSB raided the set. Only by bringing the bird carving close to his eyes could Castro appreciate the detail.

"Gina makes pictures. I help her."

Gina painting with one good hand and one eye, and restricted to her chair, was hard for Castro to imagine.

Fiona stood next to him while he examined the other items: several large seashells, a silver cup filled with acorns, and a book entitled *Mammalogy for Beginners*. On the wall behind the dresser, Fiona had tacked a rendering of a smiling black bear framed by a window.

"Jimmy gave me the shells."

She's a person, not a dog.

Castro had to work hard to keep his characters from being cartoons or mere types. He had been guilty of the same thing with these people. Neither Fiona nor the others were the people he would have scripted based on his initial appraisal.

They met John Gray outside the room.

"Gina would like you to help her prepare dinner," Gray said to Fiona, and she made for the kitchen.

"Come with me, Hume," said the young man without explanation.

Gray's room had been occupied by Brian Bergin—Papa Drake—during the filming. The disfigured man had covered the mirror above the dressing table with a sheet.

"Let's have a beer," Gray said. "Sit . . . please."

The writer recognized the red wooden chair Mabel Drake had favored in the photoplay. "I'll have to turn down the beer," Castro said.

"You don't have to turn down this beer. Root beer . . . made it myself. Fiona says it's delicious."

Gray filled a glass from one of two pitchers on his dresser and handed it to Castro; then he poured himself a glass from the other pitcher.

"I salute you," Gray said before taking a drink.

"How long have you lived here?" Castro asked.

"Almost two years. I was the first. For a few months, just me and Jeff."

Castro pointed to more than a dozen colorful birds displayed on a plastic table in a corner of the room. "Who made those?"

"I did," said Gray.

Beneath the table, Castro saw small knives, scalpels, an awl and a chisel, a magnifying glass, and several other tools he didn't recognize.

"How long have you been at it?" Castro said.

"Since I was a boy. Daddy taught me. Take one if you'd like."

Castro picked up a red cardinal and examined the work carefully, as he had Fiona's finch. He was no expert, but he recognized fine art when he saw it.

"Want to see my wooden leg? It'll cost you a dollar."

Castro grinned.

"You never drink?" Gray asked.

"I'm an alcoholic."

The artist sprouted a waggish look. "That makes two of us, but I ain't ready to quit."

"I'm not telling you to."

Gray laughed unpleasantly. "Daddy drank . . . because of me."

Castro shook his head. "Most people who drink do it for themselves. Is your father still alive?"

"Daddy killed himself when I was thirteen," the disfigured man answered. "How'd you like to have a monster for a son?"

Castro couldn't help thinking about the previous night's conversation in the parlor, Gray's escapade in town. Had this sad man been desperate enough to convince himself he could deceive the others without being discovered?

"You can't change the past," Castro said. "Your father was Gianni Grigio."

The artist jerked to attention. "How'd you learn that?"

"You left an article about him in my room."

Gray slapped his leg, got up, and refilled his glass. "Don't tell Jeff. He expects us to be more careful than that."

The man sat again, winced, and took a drink. "You ever watch *Shadow Time*?"

"I'm Ron Starling's biggest fan."

"Ever see the one with the soldier, dancer, and clown, all trapped inside a barrel. The six of us woke up one day with Red Cards, and we were in that barrel . . . all unwanted."

"Gina doesn't feel that way, and I don't think it's an act," Castro protested.

"Oh, she's authentic enough," replied Gray with an edge. "Here's how it is, Hume. You and Jeff remind me of how ugly I am, and Gina reminds me of how weak I am. Can I tell you a secret?"

But first, Gray took another hearty drink.

"I've never heard Gina question whether surviving her elimbryonation was worth it." Gray had pronounced that tongue-twisting word syllable by syllable. "I've certainly questioned whether elimination would have been preferable to this gray life."

Did the artist expect an answer or applause for his humorless pun?

Castro said, "What would these people do without you? You're Clement's right-hand man in the garden and around the set. Not to mention your art."

"We were talking about Gina," the artist intruded as if Castro's praise had been bestowed on someone else. "The elimbryonation damaged her spine and cost her a hand and an eye. How that lamb has managed to survive in this carnivorous world is one of life's great mysteries."

The two men heard Fiona cheering, and they left the room to see what had happened.

Clement had caught eight bass. Everyone except Max, who didn't eat fish, received a portion for dinner. The big man wasn't talkative, but he seemed to be much improved, though earlier in the day Castro had seen Last leaning rather heavily on his stick.

The conversation that night, no doubt affected by recent

events, was uninspired. Even the screenwriter's anecdotes about the photoplay fell flat.

In his bed that night, Castro could tell that someone had a room lamp on as the glow radiated up into the warehouse rafters.

The conversation with Gray had reminded him of the fallowness of his own art, of how unlikely he would see any of his work produced again. He wasn't sure he had the spark anymore. Every time he thought about Scarlet, he felt a mixture of regret and anger.

Before he knew it, he was out of bed and padding down the corridor in his pajamas and bare feet.

Just enough overhead light in the constable's set allowed Castro to find his way back to the brewing area.

He had carried a glass from his room. He could hear Gray's voice as if the man were standing next to him: *That makes two of us, but I ain't ready to quit.*

The first glass was delicious. The second was good, too. The next three or four—he lost count—were utilitarian.

With his back propped against the wall, Castro closed his eyes and succumbed to despondency. If these outskirters were going to be discovered by the Bureau—and they were—how would it hurt to speed up the process by opening up to Philby? He could excuse his previous lies by pleading he had been after material for a screenplay and needed more time with the Red Cards—plausible enough.

When he awoke, the room was dark. Castro lurched to his feet. He bathed his face with cold water from the washstand, but it was too late for that to have any effect.

Had he endured those four endless months for nothing? Castro Hume stumbled back to his room.

11

Offstage

Castro spent most of the next morning in bed with a sick head and an even sicker heart.

When he finally dragged himself out of bed, he still felt miserable. The only good thing was that he hadn't gotten sick in a lavatory with no ceiling, as that assuredly would have awakened the others.

One of that smart-ass Hemingway's characters said something that blazed in Castro's memory: "You can't get away from yourself by moving from one place to another."

The writer did his best to make himself presentable, but when he met Gina he was convinced she suspected he was hung over, or perhaps Gray had told her that someone had raided the beer keg, for Castro had surely made a dent in the reserves.

"Are you hungry?" she asked him.

"Perish the thought," he said in a dead tone.

"A piece of toast?"

Castro shook his aching head.

"You'll sit with me for a few minutes? You look as if you could use a cup of coffee."

The coffee helped, though not enough to give him an appetite.

Gina wore jeans and a zip-up sweater. Castro wondered how long it took this woman to do something as commonplace as dressing.

She rolled her chair to Castro's side and leaned in confidentially. "You may have noticed that John drinks."

Her candor startled him, sinking Castro into a brooding silence.

"John's obsessed with his appearance, but he never complains about the pain, and he has no pain medicine of any potency."

Her observation put Castro in mind of a doctor's visit when he had identified a lone eruption on his chest, which hurt when something rubbed against it.

"That papule is a kind of fibromatosis—not the kind that spreads, so don't worry," the doctor had told him.

A single papule, but how it had hurt whenever he touched it. He shuddered thinking of the dozens of eruptions all over Gray's body.

Gina broke into Castro's memory. "Remedies for pain come in many forms, don't they? I was in a death spiral after my father died, but I didn't give up, even when things were darkest . . . No, that's wrong. I did give up, but not for long."

She had a sixth sense for when someone was uncomfortable, as Castro was now. She refilled his cup and wheeled away.

Gina hadn't said or done much, but she had made him realize that as despondent as he was, the previous night had confirmed he liked the man who had arrived on this set far better than the man he had been four months prior.

Castro spent most of the day in his room, where he made up his mind about what he was going to do. On one occasion, when someone knocked on the door, he didn't answer, and whoever it was went away.

He was convinced these people would soon be discovered, but not because of him. When no one was around, Castro carried his packed bag to the Plebeolan. What had Cooperwasser told him? "The curtain has its moment. Don't belabor the scene."

More than anything, he wanted to speak to Sarah before he left, but what was he supposed to say? That he was sorry he might have led the SSB here? Afraid that every day he remained increased the danger? That the more time he spent with her, the harder it was to leave? Anyway, what did a seriously ill woman need with any man, much less someone she barely knew, and that man a wreck? Nevertheless, Castro had an idea, a desperate one, but only by returning to L.A. might this idea amount to something.

The residents were to meet in the library set that evening. Castro slipped out of his room a half hour before the group was scheduled to gather.

As he had hoped, the library was empty. For good measure, he closed the door.

On two walls were floor-to-ceiling bookcases. The shelves were tightly packed, as the director had desired when filming scenes on this set. Some of the books at eye level Castro recognized as old covers shipped here to fill shelves. Also, there were volumes Cooperwasser had stored here and never removed: *The Huron Forest: Geography, Geology, Biology* and *The Art of Suspense* by Alfred Cooperwasser, with J. A. Malecke.

Thinking of the flora and fauna of the Huron Forest, Castro compared the Red Cards hiding on the edge of the forest to the field mice in the meadow. Every time a mouse came out of its hole, it had to be on the alert for the red-tailed hawks that relentlessly patrolled the terrain from above. Castro had seen a hawk come down on a mouse like a lightning strike, first beating its beak against the scrambling creature, then carrying the limp body off, all in a matter of seconds. The mice survived because they bred fast enough to replace those taken by the hawks, but these Red Cards were too few, and the SSB were many. That cold equation foretold their inevitable fate—and his, if the hawks took him for a mouse.

The residents drifted into the library. Mice in deadly peril, perhaps, but tonight in a gregarious mood. "I'd be sorry to quarrel over it," John said to Gina, both of them grinning.

Out of nowhere, Fiona asked, "Why are you so big, Max?"

"I grew up in Texas. Everything's bigger there," the man drawled.

"If that's so, you should have been born in Alaska," said the old stork by the door.

Last stuck out his tongue at Colleen.

"Can you do something with this, Max?" said Gina, handing him a toaster.

"I'll buy a new one next time I'm in town," Clement said.

The big man shook his head. "Don't waste your money. I'll fix it."

"What if it needs parts?" protested the custodian.

"The set's filled with parts if you know what to look for, and where to look. Want me to make it fly, too?"

"Yes, Max," Fiona exclaimed. "I know you can do it."

Jumbo gave Fiona the warmest smile Castro had ever seen on the man's face. He had never witnessed such solidarity on the set when *Stars Too Bright* was being filmed. Working with actors like Kenny Marks and Letta Lane, he had spent many days walking on eggshells.

Gina said, "I have an announcement." She waited until all was quiet. "In recognition of his brave efforts on our behalf and his patience with our suspicions and annoying questions, we bestow this honorary Red Card on Castro

Hume." Gina turned to Castro and handed him a piece of cardboard on a string, colored with a red pencil and labeled with elegant calligraphy.

The man honored with this token wondered whether word had gotten around about last night's drunken episode or the travel bag he had surreptitiously stowed in the car. Was this their way of saying they didn't hold it against him?

Castro stood and bowed.

"Did you enjoy working with Claude Benson and the others?" Gina asked. Castro restrained a smile. "All of them were extremely talented . . . they told me so. Quite often."

A few seconds later, everyone either laughed or smiled. Gina wasn't finished probing. "Were you nervous writing a screenplay for a famous book?"

He sat and put the ersatz Red Card around his neck. "I knew we'd detour from the book. Cooperwasser told me he didn't want the photoplay to be gritty, but he wanted a faster pace and to keep viewers on edge."

In the doldrums as he had been all day, Castro was warmed a bit by the memory of Cooperwasser's words about his own contributions: "You knew Lynn Chambers' chapters set in the Drake children's childhood and those as adults wouldn't work in a photoplay adaptation. You sensed early on that the adaptation had to merge those two worlds while keeping the viewers' attention fixed on the more dramatic adult world."

"Do you miss those days?" asked Gina.

Castro was supposed to say he was excited about the future. That's what his former agent, who had cut him loose, would have told him to say.

"Every day," he admitted.

Castro waited until Colleen had engaged the group in a lively conversation about Michigan winters to slip out of the library. If anyone saw him leave, they would assume he was using the bathroom.

He didn't want to say goodbye. Easier to get into the car and start driving.

But as he walked toward the Plebeolan, Castro had the sense that he wasn't alone. Turning around, he saw that he was being followed.

"You're leaving!"

He waited for Fiona to catch up, then the pair continued walking together. "Don't go yet," she begged.

This was exactly what Castro had been trying to avoid. Of all people, how had Fiona discerned he was leaving?

"I don't want you to go," she murmured.

"I have to go, Fiona. Trust me."

Fiona looked dismayed, and unguardedly so. "Sarah wants you to stay," she said.

Castro stopped a few feet from the car. He didn't know what to say, so he took her by the shoulders and kissed her on the forehead. He opened the car door and sat down, telling himself this wasn't his car and this wasn't his place, but that didn't make leaving any easier.

He pulled the door closed. If he didn't hurry, the others might come looking for Fiona. She waved at him, and he waved back at her.

On his way south, Castro stopped for coffee and a snack in Tawas City. When he opened his bag to fetch a sweater, he found a folded piece of paper he hadn't packed, a copy of a birth certificate, identifying a newborn named Phiona Philby, daughter of Phiona and Edgar Philby, born at Regis Maximus Hospital in Boston.

Who had put this information in his bag, and why? Had Commander Philby managed to get at his bag? For what purpose?

He'd already paid the bill and was preparing to leave the café when a woman in her thirties with an expression that meant business slipped into the booth across from him.

"You're Castro Hume," the woman said.

Wrapped up in trying to decipher that mysterious birth certificate, Castro had already spent more time in the restaurant than he had intended.

"I know."

She took that in stride. "I was a production assistant on the set . . . Mary Fry."

Yes, Castro recalled this woman trailing Cooperwasser with coffee, pens, whatever the director needed.

"Most of them wouldn't give me the time of day. You were different."

Maybe this woman expected him to say something, but after Philby and her goons he was on guard.

"Muriel Martel was my best friend."

The name rang a bell. He thought for a minute—the local woman who had played Betty Drake's friend, the actress who had disappeared during filming.

He ordered two more cups of coffee for them.

"Satisfying Alfred Cooperwasser isn't easy," Castro complimented the woman.

"I was dependable—that's what Mr. Cooperwasser cared about most. May I tell you something?"

This had been a long day, and he had a long drive ahead of him. To set expectations, Castro said, "I'm on my way to Detroit."

"I won't keep you long, Mr. Hume. I never expected ever again to meet anyone from the photoplay. When I saw you, I couldn't pass up the chance to talk to you."

Perhaps Mary took his silence as permission to continue. "My younger sister adopted Papa Drake because our own father was cold-hearted. Remember the scene with Papa and young Oscar the night before he went to war, and the scene when Betty was confused about whether to leave for college or stay in Trillium? Papa Drake didn't tell his children what to do, he helped them make good decisions. All the while, I kept seeing a hungover Brian Bergin—my sister's beloved Papa Drake—arriving late to the set and tormenting Cooperwasser, and a haughty Karrie Zeeb, who wouldn't acknowledge that I existed."

"An occupational hazard," Castro ruefully agreed. He had been in the business long enough to be able to separate Bergin from Papa Drake, Karrie from Betty Drake, and the mercurial Kenny from the heroic Oscar Drake.

Mary smiled at Castro's observation. "My sister still talks about the photoplay. One day, Mr. Cooperwasser gave me permission to let her watch a shoot. I thought she was going to jump out of her skin."

What would Mary Fry's sister think if she spent a day with the Red Cards, following them from set to set, walking around town with Colleen? The sets had felt so real to fans of *Stars Too Bright*. What would they think about the people now undergoing their harsh realities there? Even Castro, who knew as well as anyone about photoplay illusions, had had a hard time adjusting to those . . . well, interlopers.

"Can you guess what happened to Muriel?" Mary asked him.

Castro recalled nothing more than that he had to write the woman out of the rest of the photoplay when she had missed her calls. He wouldn't mention the wolves in the woods or the bear at the window. What kind of closure would that be?

Mary said, "She disappeared, and Muriel wasn't the type

to vanish like that. I knew her my whole life. She saw *Stars* as her big break."

Mary must have recognized Castro's skepticism, because her eyes narrowed when she said, "I know something no one else knows. Maybe the police know, though they've never said anything publicly. Muriel was pregnant."

Listening to Mary Fry stirred something in Castro's memory, something that had happened while filming the photoplay, a memory he had recently revisited. The problem was, he had revisited dozens of memories in recent days. He couldn't immediately recall one that involved Muriel Martel, that small-part actress who had been overshadowed by the scene-stealing Karrie. And even if the memory reemerged, why should it have anything to do with that local actress' disappearance years ago?

"Do you think Muriel left to do something about the pregnancy, or to have the baby?"

Mary shook her head determinedly. "She was a bright girl, a striver . . . not a grasper." The woman frowned. "I'm painting a bizarre picture of Muriel. She was anything but bizarre. I think someone on the set was responsible for what happened to her. Not just anyone. Someone credible enough to convince Muriel they could help her in Hollywood. She never surfaced in Hollywood, Mr. Hume."

"She didn't tell you who this person was?"

"Muriel liked to keep secrets until she could make a big splash. She loved riddles and puzzles. When I pressed Muriel about her secret, she said, 'Here's your answer,' and gave me a numbers puzzle. It was nonsense to me."

As much as Castro had on his mind that night, how could a Ron Starling disciple resist a mystery? "Do you still have the puzzle?"

"I don't know."

"If you find the puzzle, send it to me. I'm no mathematician so don't get your hopes up," he quickly added. "Write down your phone number, and I'll let you know if I learn anything."

Mary said, "Don't waste your time with the police. They're not interested."

"Why are you interested? It's been years."

"Muriel was my friend," she said in a way that suggested no further explanation was needed.

Fortune smiled on Castro. He was able to secure the last seat on the plane, and was then moved to the first cabin when the flight was found to be oversubscribed.

After a string of hectic days, and having arrived in Detroit after midnight, he had expected to be asleep before the plane left the runway. Instead, he was drawn to the older gentleman seated next to him, neatly attired in a jacket and tie and writing a mile a minute in a tightly lined journal.

Castro's traveling companion possessed a narrow face, prominent nose, and a full head of gray hair.

Somewhat abashed by his own bedraggled appearance, Castro was, nevertheless, attracted by the man's keen attention to his journal.

"I'm a writer myself," Castro announced by way of introduction.

The elderly man surveyed Castro carefully before he replied. "I am not a writer," he said in accented English. "I am a criminologist, a forensic scientist. Locard is my name." He put an expensive looking auto-stylus into his jacket pocket. "What do you write?"

"Photoplay scripts, and I've tried my hand at stage plays. Castro Hume."

"Your credits, Monsieur?" the man cheerfully inquired.

"The screenplay for *Stars Too Bright* is my most highly regarded work," Castro answered.

Locard's eyes widened. "Ah, my daughter has encouraged me to view that film. The famous director . . . "

"Alfred Cooperwasser." Castro filled in the blank.

"Just so. Cooperwasser's *Without a Doubt* is a reasonably credible crime drama for a photoplay."

Castro didn't reveal that criminological credibility wasn't one of Coop's priorities.

"Where is your home?" Castro asked.

"Lyon, France. And yours?"

"Los Angeles."

Locard nodded. "Yet you embark from Michigan . . . forensic scientists seek to connect every thread, you see."

"I visited the *Stars Too Bright* set, not far from Lake Huron."

"I prefer the Côte d'Azur myself." Locard looked down at his journal.

"I won't interrupt your work," Castro said.

"Not at all. I was invited to address the International Criminological Society's convention in Los Angeles about a principle I've developed over many years."

A gentle bouncing of the plane commenced, causing the man and the woman across the aisle to steady their drinks.

"Would you be kind enough to explain your theory to me?" Castro asked.

"Oh, it is more than a theory," Locard responded with enthusiasm. "In essence, I am convinced that when considering a crime scene, every single contact leaves a trace." Locard raised a finger. "Simply put, the perpetrator of a crime will bring something to the crime scene and leave with something. There is no such thing as a clean crime scene or a clean perpetrator."

By this time, Castro couldn't help grasping the significance of the criminologist's principle. If, as the SSB maintained, the *Stars* set was a crime scene, he had surely left something behind and he had surely taken something away—the birth certificate, Gina's manufactured Red Card, and Gray's cardinal.

"It's a foundational principle in forensic dialectics," Locard continued.

An observation that meant nothing to Castro, but with Mary Fry fresh in his mind, he asked, "What if a crime is suspected—say a missing person—but neither the crime scene nor a body can be found?"

The steward placed a glass of red wine on Locard's tray. When the server had moved on, the criminologist whispered, "Airplane wine is always an adventure. Will you join me?"

"I've renounced Bacchus," Castro told him.

Locard shrugged and sipped his wine. "Bien sûr, an undiscovered crime scene is a more difficult challenge. The site of such a crime can often be narrowed down by considering where the missing person was last known to be, by drawing concentric circles around that location, and by identifying sites within those circles most favorable to the as yet undiscovered perpetrator. I assure you, once you have discovered the crime scene, you will also find something the perpetrator left behind."

Castro began to respond, but Locard cut him off with the single-minded fixation Castro had witnessed often enough in working with Alfred Cooperwasser. "When the crime scene evidence leads you to the perpetrator, you will surely find something he has taken away . . . whether he intended to or not."

PART II

Minerva

12

Scarlet

July, West Hollywood, California

As Scarlet strutted through the club toward Castro, all hope that she would be sympathetic evaporated. He read the opposite in her posture and the expression on her face.

The Red Garland Trio was playing smooth jazz at a volume that accommodated conversation and Industry gossip.

Castro stood and helped Scarlet into her chair. She placed a small lizard-skin handbag on the table. Castro had seen ads for these bags that changed color—a thousand if it cost a penny. At the moment, the bag was bright green.

She had yet to meet his eyes.

The interior of the Saint-Tropez sparkled with colored lights, dazzling accent pieces, and high-end furniture and fixtures. With his now-tarnished reputation, Castro had barely wheedled a reservation. Only a reminder that he had an Oscar had tipped the scales. With the passage of time, that currency was tarnishing, too.

Scarlet was already distracted, glancing around the club for familiar faces, celebrity faces, a far cry from the days when he could command her attention. She had set her sights on a large center table populated by two young leading men, Bobby Powell and Syd Kolt, a host of women, and an imageographer who had two Oscars and hadn't let them go to his head.

A white-jacketed waiter appeared at their table, and Scarlet ordered the martinis they had always enjoyed, a vodka martini for him and an Emerson for her. Castro thought he caught a whiff of cigarette smoke. Had she taken up the habit again?

Scarlet was naturally pretty and worked hard to look spectacular. She was taller than average and curvy without being fleshy, and she had done the best she could with her beady eyes. Her mane-like red hair was her best feature, and she knew it, keeping the tresses long and flowing. Her pearls were real. Castro was sure she had wanted him to see them. She was wearing a canary yellow blouse with a black silk scarf and a short black leather skirt.

Castro recalled the day he had met—rather, been smitten by—Scarlet di Roma. Claude Benson had hosted a *Stars Too Bright* pre-production party at his estate in the Hills. Scarlet had been one of a handful of ingénues Claude had invited to spice up the event. Castro had already signed on to compose the screenplay and was considered an up-and-coming talent.

For the next three years they had been a couple, had even brushed up against the A-List when Castro won his Academy Award. Scarlet took good advantage of the bright lights, and Castro had helped her secure roles.

The actress was older now, but as he looked at her across the table, he had to admit that she had protected her assets. No longer an ingénue, Scarlet was a serviceable actress with steady work in supporting roles, not bad for a small-town kid from North Carolina. If Francie Gumm walked the rim of the volcano, Scarlet had been satisfied with a view of the inferno while keeping her distance from the hot lava.

Her stunning red tresses bounced when she turned back to face him. "Here I am," she said.

"You look lovely, Brenda," he said to her.

"I'm Scarlet now . . . to you, too. I can't stay long, you know."

The sad truth was that Scarlet had been a provisional lover. "You told me that on the phone," Castro demurred. "I was hoping you could help me with something."

"If this *something* has to do with finding you work, you're wasting your time."

He bristled at her hauteur. "How many calls did I make for you when you were trying to break into the business?"

She waved her hand as if a fly were pestering her. "You got your pound of flesh. I don't owe you anything."

Making Scarlet angry wouldn't help with the request Castro intended to make. This woman had always possessed a quick temper and an acid tongue, but in recent months, she had become a virago, at least where Castro was concerned. He had planned to ask if she would find Sarah a place to stay in Los Angeles; that was, if Castro could talk Sarah into coming. He had a now-or-never sense about getting Sarah Pasternak off the *Stars* set.

As if she could read his mind, Scarlet said, "So, you went back to that set. Why would you do such a thing? Makes you look . . . I don't know . . . desperate."

"Maybe I am desperate."

"If you are, you don't need to let everyone else know."

"Chandler is erratic," Castro countered, "That hasn't hurt his reputation."

She laughed scornfully. "You may have his vices, but you're no Chandler. So, what do you want, or is this about bantering with a willing fool?"

"Whose line is that? Your new boyfriend's?"

Her eyes flashed, and she took a healthy sip from her glass. "You haven't touched your drink, Castro. Turned over a new leaf?"

Out of the corner of his eye, the screenwriter saw a familiar pear-shaped figure enter the club, accompanied by a woman who was shielded by her companion. As the new arrival turned toward him, Castro could see that it was indeed Alfred Cooperwasser. The director recognized Castro at the same time and made for their table.

"*Mister* Hume," Cooperwasser said jovially while maintaining that indolent expression Castro had come to know so well. "We haven't heard much from you lately."

The famed director of *Vertiginous* and *Without a Doubt* wore his trademark copper-colored bow tie. Not knowing how to respond, Castro opted for, "You know Scarlet, I think."

"Yes, . . . of course." Cooperwasser turned to the woman who accompanied him and said, "My niece, Dana Philby. One of your admirers."

Castro stood and shook Philby's hand with a simulated air of cordiality. Her plastic face was impassive. Castro invited the two to join them. Cooperwasser politely declined. The director had taken a step away when Philby said, "Actually, Mr. Hume and I met in Michigan. I was on assignment at the time."

"Dana does something for the state," Cooperwasser explained, giving Castro a mischievous glance. "A steadier paycheck than our business."

Holding an empty cocktail glass in each hand, Syd Kolt loudly hailed a passing waiter. "The tide's gone out!"

Cheers erupted. Kolt bowed.

"Did you enjoy your stay on the set?" Philby asked Castro.

Before he could answer, Cooperwasser cut in. "Don't tell me you made a pilgrimage to that old haunt. A long way to travel, though perhaps it will do you good . . . dear boy," he added in a conciliatory tone.

"There wasn't much to see or do," Castro answered the woman.

Looking grave, she said, "We still think people are residing illegally on that set. You're sure you didn't see anyone except for the caretaker?"

Philby hadn't taken long to dispense with the small talk. "No one" was Castro's reply.

"We hear all kinds of things that aren't true," she remarked.

Was she referring to an informant who had directed the agents to the set or to Castro's denying he had seen anyone? Nothing in her face or voice revealed the answer.

Castro could feel Scarlet tugging on his slacks.

Philby said, "You have my number if you think of anything."

"We must go, my dear," Cooperwasser said to his niece. His eyes narrowed when he addressed Castro. "Enjoyed seeing you again, Hume, and you, Miss di Roma."

As that odd couple made their way across the club, Scarlet was staring at Castro with an ambiguous expression. "That trip to Michigan didn't enhance your reputation in this town."

"That's not why I went," he said.

Scarlet shook her head disdainfully. "He didn't say a word about working with you again. You're a long way from that runway. Too long to be haughty. Drink that martini. It might do you some good."

Drinking the martini to the dregs was exactly what he felt like doing.

Red Garland broke into a jaunty rendition of *One O'Clock Jump*. An older woman wearing a multicolored fashion toque who had obviously had several drinks too many was dancing solo in front of the bandstand.

"What do you want from me, Scarlet?" Castro asked in a pleading tone.

"Not a thing. You invited me here, remember? You used to have talent." With a smirk, she said, "When snow melts, it goes downhill . . . right into the sewer."

"So do cockroaches," Castro fired back.

Scarlet practically jumped to her feet, grabbed her bag—now an orange-red hue—and walked away without looking back.

No matter the provocation, his words had been shockingly indecent. If she had delayed her departure, he might have apologized.

More than a few eyes followed the actress' progress to the door, and when she arrived at the red canopied entrance, the maître d' and a lithe Syd Kolt, who had darted from his table to the door, showed her out—a gesture that might compensate Scarlet for indulging Castro.

Even at that distance, her coquetry was evident.

"I've seen the backs of too many façades," Castro mumbled. He thought for a minute and forced a smile. "Including my own."

He could see the maître d' eyeing him, as if to hurry him from the table. What had made him think Scarlet would do anything that wasn't in her own interests? The difficulty of persuading her to meet him should have been ample evidence.

Despite the glamour of the club, the fresh band, and the

apparent bonhomie of the guests, an aura of joylessness saturated this place. Castro was tempted to consume the martini, and several more, but the Saint-Tropez wasn't the place to get blitzed unless you had a celebrity posse to escort you home.

As the evening had turned out, however, Scarlet had been a sideshow to the appearance of Dana Philby. He couldn't believe the agent's presence in the club was a coincidence, or that her questions were as innocuous as she made them seem. She was here, he told himself, because he was here, an idea that produced a frisson of fear.

Castro shifted his attention to the bar, an altogether inadequate name for that mahogany and stained-glass edifice.

Something Gina had said encouraged him: *I did give up, but not for long.* Leaving the martini behind, he vacated his table and found an open seat at the bar. The pretty bartender who made her way toward him flashed a smile. "What can I get you?"

"Cranberry juice on the rocks. I'm hiding from government agents. I need all my wits."

She laughed at that. "Are you a provocateur?"

"Not the dangerous kind," he replied as she went to get his drink.

Today, Castro had received notice his Uncle Pat had died. He had immediately bought the most impersonal card he could find and mailed it to his Aunt Miranda. He hadn't written a word in the card, just printed his name. Still, weaponizing his response hadn't satisfied him as he had expected it would.

What came to his mind when he had posted the card was his aunt's disparaging rant about Extraordinary Designation Card holders.

"They're people like us," the boy Castro had protested, knowing what he did about his dead sister.

"To a certain extent," Miranda had equivocated.

"Here you go," the bartender said to him. She had a cheery voice that would be an asset for a woman tending bar. "Is Scarlet di Roma your girlfriend?"

He was surprised to have been asked a personal question. "Once upon a time."

"That was a hasty exit."

Castro put a hand over his heart. "Heartbroken but undaunted," he gallantly said.

She grinned. "Are you in the film business, too?"

"A screenwriter." He wanted to add that he had scripted *Stars Too Bright*, but that always sounded so pretentious.

She stepped toward a man at the other end of the bar who was waving a hand at her.

Scarlet had played her cards well. Theirs had always been a transactional relationship, and she had expressed it better than he ever could: *You got your pound of flesh*. What Mary Fry had said about Muriel Martel reflected a depth of friendship Castro had never experienced with Scarlet.

If he was smart, he would forget about Sarah and the Red Cards and lean on his few Hollywood friends until he found work.

13

The Obsolete Man

Every time Castro gazed at the gold-plated statuette on the shelf, he recalled snippets of that intoxicating awards night. This time, the memory was especially vivid, perhaps because he had seen Scarlet and Alfred Cooperwasser so recently, or perhaps because the likelihood of being nominated for, much less winning, another Oscar was so remote.

Nevertheless, on the plane back to California and every day since, the writer had been working furiously on the script he had conceived in Michigan, inspired by the residents of the *Stars Too Bright* set.

Tonight, however, he was attending to different business. Spread out on his all-purpose table were engineering drawings for the *Stars* set that confirmed what Castro had suspected. Before actors and crew had arrived, a tunnel had been constructed from the warehouse to the woods.

Two days after their encounter at the Saint-Tropez, Castro had visited Cooperwasser. With some prodding, the director had admitted he had built the tunnel so he could amaze the cast and crew with his vanishing act. With time on his hands and an exploratory bent, Clement must have discovered the tunnel and converted it into an emergency refuge for the Red Cards.

There it was, as plain as day on the drawings, traversing the warehouse at a depth of fifteen feet, the access hatch located inside the dining room set, covered with Cooperwasser's own rug.

As Castro was leaving the director's elegant studio office, he had been stopped in his tracks by Cooperwasser's words.

"You're the second person to ask about those plans in the past week."

"Who else is interested?" Castro had turned back and asked.

"Play dumb if you must. A friendly warning, Mr. Hume: some people you don't want to cross."

With more enthusiasm than he felt, Castro had said, "I'm good for a fight, and I'll be looking for work if I return in one piece."

"I'm sorry to say I don't think you'll return in one piece," Cooperwasser had fired back. "As to work, Starling knows of our acquaintance. He called me and said he'd like you to pay him a visit. Your time would be better spent with him than batting at hornets' nests."

Castro was dumbfounded. "Did he tell you why?"

"No, and I didn't ask. I've passed along his message. Do with it what you will."

If Cooperwasser's warning wasn't bad enough, Castro was running out of money, and he didn't have to compare his current lodgings to Claude Benson's home, or even to the Beverly Hills apartment he had lived in after *Stars Too Bright* was released, to recognize that he had come down in the world. All he had to do was look at this dingy rent-in-advance flat in an insalubrious corner of Los Angeles to know that. Moreover, he would have had less than this if not for Cooperwasser's beneficence in the form of a small royalty. Most nights, he didn't leave the room after dark because the streets weren't safe, and when he did, legging it from the apartment to his car was fraught with anxiety.

Using his index finger, he traced the tunnel from the warehouse to an exit manhole about fifty yards inside the wood line, telling himself it couldn't have been easy for some of the Red Cards to climb or be lowered down the ladder into that narrow tunnel when the SSB arrived on the set.

Cooperwasser's warning meant Dana Philby now knew how the trick had been worked. Clement and the others would have to be alerted, if Castro wasn't already too late.

At the end of his table was the envelope he had received from Mary Fry, containing one sheet of paper with numbers inside a square.

4	_	2
3	5	7
_	1	_

This was Muriel Martel's puzzle, which Mary suggested might shed light on the actress' disappearance. Castro's few minutes with the puzzle earlier that day hadn't produced any inspiration. He never did have a head for numbers. He could barely keep track of his steadily declining bank balance.

He rolled up the drawings and stashed them under his bed. Why was he procrastinating? Why couldn't he act?

He didn't hear the first knock. The second was louder. He called out, "Who is it?"

"SSB Commander Philby," said the voice on the other side.

He fought down the tasteless meat pie he had eaten for dinner with a hard swallow. "What do you want?" he called out.

"Let me in, Hume."

Castro opened the door. She took in the room. The contemptuous look on her face told him how unimpressed she was with his lodgings.

What Castro couldn't have imagined—what this woman hid from years of practice—were the powerful emotions these shabby quarters evoked in her.

Dana Philby was severely tailored in a dark gray jacket, light gray slacks, and a buttoned-up blouse with a string tie. She wore no observable makeup. Her hair was almost invisible beneath a black brimless cap.

From behind her back, the SSB commander produced an unopened bottle of wine and set it down on the table. "I've never seen an Oscar up close," she said, closing the door.

Castro gave the statue a quick look. By the time he turned around, she had opened the bottle.

"Get a couple glasses" sounded more like an order than a request.

He went to the kitchenette, came back with one glass and set it in front of her. She filled the glass and pushed it toward him.

Temptation was tugging at him like a physical force, as it had that night in his room on the set.

"Ever thought of pawning your Oscar?" Philby asked.

She had him exactly where she wanted him. He might have been contending with an Olympian goddess for the despair he felt at that moment.

"What right do you have to interrogate me?" he asked defiantly.

"Harboring criminals is serious business . . . for collaborators, too. What do you know about a tunnel beneath the warehouse?"

If the best he could do was tread water, so be it. For Sarah, he told himself.

"What warehouse?"

She made a dismissive sound. "I wouldn't make light of it if I were you. My uncle reluctantly admitted you had an interest in engineering drawings for the set."

As distracted as Castro already was, he couldn't afford to dwell on his fear of the commander searching his apartment and finding the engineering drawings, Mary Fry's letter from Michigan that contained Muriel's puzzle, and Gray's wooden cardinal.

He gave himself a mental shake. "I can't tell you anything," he insisted.

"You've been sending scientific journals to one Jefferson Clement. He isn't a scientist," she said.

Even if Castro knew about the Red Cards, why would SSB Commander Philby need him? Had this become a personal vendetta?

"You're obsolete," Philby heckled him. "Everyone I've talked to says so."

Starling's *Obsolete Librarian* came back to him in a rush, a man charged with a capital offense for owning books proscribed by the state. Quoting the librarian in the show, Castro said, "No man is obsolete."

She fixed that basilisk stare on him. "Tell me something, Hume. Are you a melancholic drunk or a raver?"

Already seething on the inside, Castro set himself to wait her out.

Presently, she clasped her hands and said, "Do you have any idea how much trouble I can make for you? Tell me what you know about Muriel Martel."

Even if Philby had read Mary Fry's letter, Muriel's name

had never been mentioned. Why would that actress' disappearance spell trouble for him? "I might have spoken to her a few times on the set."

She flashed some teeth, and said, "And off the set? We've been told you knew her quite well."

So, that was Philby's gambit, connecting him to Muriel, and maybe the actress' disappearance—a murder charge, a capital offense.

Was she bluffing? He had told Cooperwasser he was good for a fight. What kind of fight? Castro said, "When we filmed Oscar Drake at the train station, heading off to war in the pouring rain, it was sunny and ninety-three degrees on the set. All the Drakes were wearing wool coats. The crew was dousing the tin canopy with fire hoses. I can separate theater from reality."

Dana Philby stood, gave him an ugly smile, and exited the apartment.

White-faced and trembling, Castro waited a minute, then, he swept the glass of wine off the table. The glass rattled across the floor intact until it shattered against the wall. Seconds later, he sent the wine from the bottle gurgling down the drain.

14

Scorpion of a Script

August

"I wouldn't touch that scorpion of a script for all the tea in China," Ba Jin erupted. "Your Oscar earned you a reading . . . a *partial* reading. Don't come back until you have something serious."

Ba Jin tossed the draft at Castro. The manuscript landed on the floor in a jumble. Since Ba was known as one of the most audacious producers in Hollywood, this frigid reception gave Castro scant hope his script would receive a sympathetic reading from anyone.

"What do you suggest?" Castro asked the producer.

"Shred it, if you care about your career. Is that plain enough?" said Ba loftily. "This script would incense all the wrong people. You must know that."

Castro had a lot he wanted to say, but clearly Ba Jin's mind was made up.

The producer lowered his voice. "I shouldn't be telling you this, but I was visited by the SSB, and they were interested in you."

When Castro didn't reply, Ba Jin leaned in. "SSB, Castro. Talk about provoking the wrong people. I guarantee they aren't vetting you for an award. . . . Are you listening?"

Ba bent down, picked up the script, and handed it to Castro, clutching the writer's wrist with his other hand. "I hear you're still getting crazy high. Better knock it off if you want to work again."

"Who told you that? The SSB?"

Ba didn't have to answer for Castro to know he had guessed correctly. Was there any doubt the SSB were gaslighting him, spearheaded by Philby?

"I'm sober. I was sober when I composed this screenplay."

"You look like you've been buried alive," the producer said.

"I've been working nonstop on the script. I haven't had time to eat or sleep."

Not so great an exaggeration.

Ba shrugged. "I have a project coming up, if you can still write. See me in a few months. In the meantime, don't get on the wrong side of the Bureau."

Castro left the producer's office gripping his manuscript as if it were actually worth something. He saw a large man, not big enough for a Red Card, prance across the street. He couldn't help remembering Jumbo's observation: *Everyone knows fat guys make the best dancers*.

15

Mantle

Castro was admitted to the house by a stocky, white-shirted man in his thirties who showed him into a lamplit room where an emaciated old man sat in front of a dark TV.

"Thanks for coming," murmured Ron Starling in a labored voice. "Have a seat."

Castro's host motioned him to a duplicate of the Shaker dining chair the old man sat on.

He labored to recognize the titan who had inspired his life's work in this shriveled-up shell of a man. Gone were the sport coat, the tie and white shirt, the earnest expression, and the monotone voice that had once cut to the heart. The day was pleasant, but all the windows were closed and curtained. In addition to the TV, the room contained two side-by-side bookcases packed with a jumble of books, bound scripts, and magazines. The wood floor needed a lot of work, so did the walls and ceiling.

Castro said, "How are you feeling, sir?"

"Awful," the man rasped. "And cut the sir crap. You think staying alive ought to be my only project, don't you? I don't have time to worry about staying alive. I'm planning to put sticks in some eyes."

"Like the old days?" Castro cautiously returned.

"Exactly, with new material." Starling's words were accompanied by a struggle to take in some air. The effort produced several panting breaths.

Rattling around in Castro's brain was the thought that this might not be Starling at all, that the real Ron Starling was dead or had been moved out of the house. Castro had seen enough of the SSB to know they weren't beyond that kind of duplicity. The person across from him could be an actor. Who was to say this wasn't a Philby scheme to trip him up, to deceive him into telling what he knew?

Maybe suspicion showed on his face, because his host said, "How do you know you can trust me?"

He beckoned Castro with a crooked finger. Lowering his high collar, Starling revealed a trach tube in his throat with a tiny device at the terminus. "They put oxygen in there to help me breathe. The engineer who invented that little gadget made gazillions—airtight when closed, modulation, precise backpressure control all in one device. Talking's the least of my problems."

"There can't be much demand for those . . . ah . . . "

With weary eyes, Starling said, "As it happens, plenty of demand in androids and robots when it comes to simulating human speech." Starling brought his forefinger close to the tiny device, and said in a hissed whisper, "Those goons would have to go to a lot of trouble to fake that. But I like your attitude, kid. You'll need big stones if you decide to join me . . . Bring that chair closer so we can talk without shouting."

Starling retrieved a cigarette from his shirt pocket and produced an unadorned stainless steel lighter. If everything else in the room appeared wanting, the lighter delivered a bold flame on the first click.

"Lamps are going out all over this country. Our children's children may not see them lit again in their lifetimes."

Castro took up Starling's theme with vigor. "*Any state*

that doesn't recognize the worth, the dignity, the rights of man, is obsolete."

"Sounds familiar," said Starling.

"Why me?" Castro asked.

His host smoked a moment before answering. "This has nothing to do with *Stars Too* . . . whatever—or your Oscar. Coop said he spoke with you at the Saint-Tropez."

The white-shirted attendant came into the room, and Starling went silent while the man spread a rug over the old man's lap.

"Do you have a Red Card?" Castro asked, once the attendant had left the room.

"Not me," Starling said with a wave of his cigarette. "They're only for schmucks. The Bureau isn't all-powerful . . . not yet. They're like rats in a basement that know if they overrun the whole house they'll start a war they might not win. Going after people in the pantheon of the Cosmopolis"—he patted his chest—"shines a light on those rats."

The *pantheon of the Cosmopolis*—was Castro's Oscar the only thing keeping him from the full wrath of the SSB?

"Mind if I smoke?"

Since this was his hero's second cigarette, Castro didn't think the man expected an answer.

Starling said, "What I want is a script that'll do the SSB in the eye. Put it on Mars, or in ancient Carthage, wherever. Think you can deliver something in a month?"

"One month?"

"Buck had no problem with three scripts a month," Starling shot back, referring to his former collaborator.

"I'm no Buck Addison, not even close. You should know I haven't written anything of consequence in years."

"So I've heard." The old man brought a hand all the way

to his lips before realizing the cigarette was perched on the edge of the chair. He managed a devilish little grin. "Do you think the Muses reveal their secrets for free? And the more they reveal, the steeper the toll. That's how it works. So, what do you say?"

"I'm already working on something, and I didn't have to put it on Mars." Without revealing his real-life inspiration, Castro supplied a sixty-second synopsis of the story.

"Hmm, what are you calling it?"

"Brighter Stars."

"That's no stick-in-the-eye title."

"I figure it will draw in—"

"Scrap the title. If you're worried the story won't draw them in, you're telling the wrong story. Give 'em both barrels! Don't hold anything back."

Starling waved his cigarette. "I'm putting my mantle on your shoulders, so don't let me down."

"You're sick—"

Starling coughed a smoky laugh. "That's a creative way of describing someone with one foot in the grave and the other tottering on the edge."

"And I'm a pariah in this town . . . " Castro hesitated for a moment.

"Go on."

"What makes you think we can pull this off? Who's going to finance the show?"

"Finance the project I have in mind? Not the Ba Jins of the world. Maybe I can pawn an Emmy. How about your Oscar?"

"Your Emmys and my Oscar wouldn't buy us a week of production, and you know it."

"Don't sweat the details, kid. In the beginning, Buck and I did *Shadow Time* on a shoestring. The story's what matters, not the bells and whistles."

"And good acting," Castro added.

"If you say so."

Starling rang a little bell. The attendant soon entered the room with a new pack of cigarettes. After the man had gone, Starling said, "Mark knows what I need before I ask him. Like that diabolical kid in Bixby's story."

The tobacco-stained fingers that peeled the package open were like little claws. "If you haven't guessed, this stick-in-the-eye business can be thankless work. Do I look like a happy man? The same question Gianni asked me before he pretended to join the blackshirts and was murdered when they found him out." Starling shook his head. "Hell of an artist, Gianni was."

Castro jerked to attention. "Gianni Grigio committed suicide."

"That's the official story, that Gianni was despondent about his son's condition. A pack of lies! He loved the boy —*'Mi tesoro.'*" Starling's face softened for a moment.

But his hands were trembling, needing both to hold the cigarette steady. Castro couldn't stand to see him in so desperate a condition. "What can I do to help you?"

"Not a thing. Nothing of use to any self-respecting White Card in this miserable body."

"What's a White Card?" asked Castro.

Starling deposited cigarette ash into a copper tray—somewhat the worse for wear—at his feet. "A subject for another day. In the meantime, we have a deadline, and mine is imminent."

"I'm going to Michigan," the writer said. "You may not hear from me for a while. A script expedition, but keep it to yourself."

Starling put a finger to his lips, leaned forward, put his mouth to Castro's ear, and whispered, "Mark is SSB. Put this in your pocket . . . right now."

A handwritten card with a name and address: *Charles Weems, Providence Hospital, Detroit.*

Phrase by phrase, Starling fought for breath. "Red Card Underground Railroad. Cancer's his specialty."

"Why are you giving me this?"

Castro's hero gave him that *Shadow Time* into-the-camera look, cigarette and all. "Don't lose that card, don't let it out of your hands."

16

The Reptile World

Castro had spent two full days going from studio to studio, mansion to mansion, sitting in dingy waiting rooms or fancy parlors for fifteen minutes or less with producers and directors who had agreed to meet with him only because Cooperwasser and Berkowitz had gone to bat for him. Two of those Hollywood princes had offered a glimmer of hope of the most ephemeral kind that dissipated after considering all of their ifs and whens.

Castro's car was a symbol of the futility of his quest for a new screenwriting assignment. Even the studio gatekeepers refused him entry until they confirmed that Castro had appointments with their moguls.

If Scarlet had followed him around, he guessed, she would have been highly amused.

Returning to his apartment, he had no more clarity about the path he would take—persistence in seeking work or returning to the set and collaborating with Starling—than before.

Of all things, Scarlet's lizard-skin handbag came to mind at the moment he pulled into the apartment lot.

He had met plenty of people in this town who were much like lizards and had done well enough for themselves. They changed colors at need; were adept at concealing themselves at the first sign of danger; went about their business in an efficiently self-interested manner; and made good, even lavish, livings without arousing the ire of Hollywood vipers, much less birds of prey like Dana Philby.

Alfred Cooperwasser, a man Castro respected, and Ba Jin, someone who knew his way around this town—one could say a lizard who had made himself into a grander reptile—had encouraged Castro to seek cover from those deadly birds of prey. Starling would have him charge into the fray, but Starling was practically dead, so what did that man have to lose?

Hadn't that old rake of a comic, Julius, said he would rather be a lecherous lizard than a limping lion?

The calculus was simple, wasn't it? The reptile world promised success, the esteem of people who mattered, protective coloration from Philby and her kind—much more than the soul-crushing room behind his apartment door.

Nearby, sirens sounded. Castro stepped inside and double-locked the door behind him.

17

Revelations

September

Castro had hoped to sleep on the night flight to Detroit, but the plane had passed through two violent fronts. Worn out by the time the plane landed, he stopped for coffee several times on the long drive north.

This time, Clement didn't invite Castro to leave. Was it the writer's imagination, or had the custodian gotten thinner and grayer in the three months Castro was in California?

Walking toward the warehouse, Castro asked, "Any more SSB visits?"

Clement shook his head.

"Back to normal?"

Clement stopped walking. "Gina's dead."

The news hit Castro like a kick in the gut. Except for the journals he had sent to Sarah via Clement, he had not been in contact with the Red Cards.

"Died in her sleep three weeks ago. Fiona found her. They're a resilient bunch, but this was hard."

Castro could tell the woman's death had been hard on the site manager, too.

The two men made their way to the library, where Fiona raced across the room and hugged Castro as if she would never let go. "Gina died. We buried her in the forest."

Colleen was also in the room, wearing a jacket and a hat.

The old woman glared at Castro, and said, "Why did you come back?"

Too complicated a question to answer in a few words, so he didn't try.

"Walk with me," Colleen insisted.

"Have something to eat first," Clement advised Castro.

The writer shook his head and followed Colleen to the door.

Clement called out, "I'll put your bag in your old room and leave a plate in the kitchen."

Colleen retrieved a black shoulder cape from her room and draped it over her jacket. As indomitable as this old woman was, it was easy to forget she was ninety-three. He had to keep an eye on her.

Approaching the warehouse exit, Colleen said, "The shepherd boy come to save us from the Philistines? A lot of sad faces since Gina died. You're not afraid to walk, are you?"

"Should I be?"

Colleen set a brisk pace. When they reached Main Street, she kept on walking to the end of the pavement, where she turned and started back.

Castro was sure his friend had something to say, but she apparently needed time. In spite of her bold front, he could tell that Colleen had been much shattered by Gina's death. So, he broke the silence. "You came here from Texas."

"Waco. Lived there for ninety-one years."

"Married?"

She shook her head. "Had a niece and nephew I was close to . . . in their sixties now." Colleen stopped and gripped Castro's hand. "I'm glad to see you, but do me a favor and get the hell out of here. You're no shepherd boy hero, and the SSB have an army of giants."

Off she went again. Weary as he was, Castro was determined to match her stride for stride.

She laughed. "That was some trip north with Max. We bonded. Now, reading him is hard."

He wasn't interested in Last. "Was Gina sick before she died?" he asked her.

"She wouldn't have told us if she was. I don't think she was suffering any more than she had been. The day before she died was like any other day."

"I know about the tunnel."

She glanced at him. "Do you? The day the SSB showed up we went down that hatch like beetles into a dry drain. Even the June bug."

"The SSB knows about the tunnel, too. They'll stop the drain next time."

Colleen shrugged, but Castro could tell the news had shaken her.

"You might be surprised to hear I'm proud of my Red Card. I had to earn it by living ninety years, and when I got to ninety, I was spry enough to go on the lam—me, an old maid! We'll go cross-country for a bit, along the wood line. Watch your step. The moles are busy here. Ever been in those woods?"

"Once, and that was enough."

"Do tell."

"Some other time."

"All right. Let me tell you a story."

The old woman started to choke up. Pretending not to notice, Castro gave her time to compose herself.

"My nephew and his wife had a son. For the first seven years of his life, Joshua stayed with me several days a week. I was no spring chicken then, and I was terrified at first, but I came to cherish my time with him. He called me Auntie

Collie, and in many ways we were like mother and son. Oh, how many grand things we did together, Joshua and I. I later learned that my nephew and his wife were divorcing. She moved and re-married. I never saw Joshua again. Well, . . . that was hard. Every day I wonder where he is and how he's doing. I wonder if he remembers his Auntie Collie."

Castro said, "You loved him. No one forgets that."

"I hope you're right. Afterward, my heart was like a stone in a cold stream."

She saw his look of concern and quickly added, "I was young and pretty once. It's true! My boyfriend wanted to marry me. We lived together for a year, a scandal in our little town. In those days, I thought I could do better. One night. . . . "

She stopped speaking in mid-sentence. Castro waited.

"One night, a young girl came to me in a dream. I've never forgotten her face. Soon after that dream, I moved on from my boyfriend, and here I am, an old maid."

"Not that way," he said, taking hold of her arm and steering her clear of ankle-high brambles. Never had Colleen looked so bent and fragile.

"Gina reminded me of her, Castro."

"Of whom?"

"The girl in my dream." She stifled a sob, looked away, and said, "It'll be owl time soon. You must be famished. How selfish of me to drag you out after your long trip."

"I missed you" was all he said. But she was right. He was famished. As soon as they returned to the warehouse, Castro devoured the sandwiches the custodian had left out before he joined the others in the library.

Sarah was seated at the table, along with Last, Gray, and Colleen. Fiona was fingering the spines of books on the shelves, one after another. Clement stood by the door.

Castro took the empty chair next to Sarah. He keenly felt the hole Gina had left, but this was no time for sentiment. "Commander Philby is obsessed with you all," he said. "She pressed me hard in California. She knows about the tunnel."

"Is that why you came back?" asked Sarah stiffly. "To warn us?"

They expected Castro to answer her. They were all looking at him, including Clement. What was he supposed to say, that she, Sarah Pasternak, a woman he hardly knew, was the reason he had come back? "I came back to help you."

"You're a marked man," Gray said with evident consternation. "You told us that the last time."

"That means the SSB know you're here," added Last.

"Then why haven't they pounced?" asked Sarah.

How much should he reveal? At that very moment, he was fingering Dr. Weems' card in his pocket. "Because they're afraid of something," he said.

"Afraid of us?" Last loudly scoffed.

"Yes . . . and of me. We have to find out why Philby is afraid of us and use it against her."

"That ought to be easy enough," Last returned in his mocking voice.

"He's in as much trouble as we are," Clement admonished Last. "You need rest, Hume. And Gina's sudden death has dragged us all down. We'll talk again tomorrow."

On his way to bed, the writer stopped at Gina's closed door. On an impulse, he opened the door and went into her room.

During production, these had been Letta Lane's quarters. Could he imagine two more different occupants than Letta and Gina?

The first thing he noticed was the absence of a bed.

The room was uncluttered, undoubtedly to accommodate her wheelchair. Against one wall stood two night tables with pillows on top, separated by about three feet. On another wall, was a handcrafted bookcase, a pretty piece of furniture that held several dozen volumes, including a hardcover edition of *Stars Too Bright*.

Next to the bookcase was a prop from the photoplay, Oscar Drake's officer's chest. On the front was stenciled: LIEUT OSCAR DRAKE.

The other piece of furniture in the room was an old six-drawer dresser, with a votive candle on top and a hand-lettered word on the white wall immediately above the candle: AMNOS.

Fiona had said that Gina painted, but there were no pictures in the room.

"Ah!" Castro exclaimed, turning back to the two tables crowned with pillows. Just enough space remained between those short tables for Gina to back in her wheelchair and then rest her head on one pillow or the other.

He went to the bookcase and removed Lynn Chambers' novel, surprised to find his screenplay next to it. On an impulse, he opened the novel to a random page, the scene where Betty Drake gave the telegram announcing Oscar's death on the battlefield to her brother, Stephen.

> "This can't have happened," Stephen insisted volubly. "Oscar was indestructible. Ever since he was a boy. You remember that fall from the top of the Founders Tree." Stephen Drake tried to laugh but the sound was plaintive. "This message is a lie."

Castro sought that same memorable scene in his screenplay, the final version he had argued out with Claude Benson, and then Cooperwasser.

STEPHEN DRAKE: "I don't believe it . . . I refuse to. Not Oscar. Anyone but our Hercules. He fell thirty feet and not a scratch."

STEPHEN LAUGHS DISDAINFULLY

STEPHEN (ENRAGED): "Has Mother seen this telegram? I swear someone's going to pay for this!"

Castro returned the book and the screenplay to the shelf, closed Gina's door behind him, and went to his own room. Clement had filed down the burr on the door handle, and Castro had wiped it clean of blood before he left the set, but a pea-sized brown spot remained on the floor where a drop of his blood had fallen on the night when he cut his hand.

The next morning, Sarah greeted him in the kitchen with a blasé smile. A few seconds later, she said, "You know it was foolish . . . stupid to come back. You can't do anything if they invade the set."

"Ron Starling said they prefer to leave celebrities alone," he half-heartedly responded. "Is there any coffee?"

"Who says you're a celebrity?" she chided, filling his cup without looking at him.

One sip, and he felt better, the reason he loved coffee. "I read about you when I was in L.A. People say you're one of the top mammalogists in the world."

"People *used* to say," Sarah corrected him.

Her attitude suggested he had come back for nothing. The night he had surreptitiously left the set, Fiona had told him that Sarah wanted him to stay. Castro saw no evidence of this—just the opposite.

"How are you, Sarah?"

She looked away for a moment before answering, "What do you want to know?"

"Are you sick?"

"You know I'm sick, Castro. I told you I have terminal cancer. I'm dying."

"Is it affecting you yet? . . . I mean, physically?"

In the blink of an eye, Sarah was struggling to control her emotions. She moaned and wiped her tearing eyes with a sleeve. After a deep breath, she said, "Yes."

That one word froze Castro's heart. He wanted to ask, "How badly?" but checked himself. "Thank you for telling me," he said. "I care. I've been thinking about you." He had been doing much more than that on Sarah's behalf the past three months, and he wanted to learn more; but he had pressed Sarah hard enough about this painful subject.

Apart from reddened eyes, Sarah had recovered herself. She carried her plate and utensils to the counter and hurriedly left the kitchen.

Over time, Castro had adopted the Hollywood mentality without even noticing it. Few in the industry could resist determining a person's status—not to say value—by physical beauty, attire, and possessions. Eccentric high achievers, like Cooperwasser and Starling, could overcome shortcomings in appearance and acquisitive zeal, but such as these were few and far between in Castro's world. Sarah, for whom he was taking dire risks, and who may not even think well of him, was a nobody by Hollywood standards.

As downcast as Castro was, brooding about Sarah would not help him or her. He had returned to the set to take action—scary action—on behalf of Sarah and the others.

He hurriedly consumed a bowl of cereal and an apple before knocking on John Gray's door.

"Come ahead," Gray called out.

The writer was no sooner inside the room than Gray said, "I don't care what the others say, I'm glad you're back."

"Even though I raided your beer?" Castro scanned Gray's bird table, now empty.

Gray wore his old gardening trousers, though Castro had learned this didn't mean the man had been working in the garden.

"I talked to someone in L.A. who told me Gianni Grigio loved his son," Castro nervously said. "This person doesn't believe Grigio committed suicide."

Gray sat down hard on the bed, as if his legs had given out. The artist lowered his head and put his hands to his face. When he finally looked up, the eruptions were redder than usual. "Do you trust this person?" he asked.

"More than I trust myself."

Gray's mouth formed a sly smile.

"Daddy was a handsome man. Everyone said so."

Castro tried to imagine Gray's face if all the blemishes were removed. It would be strikingly handsome.

The young man's features hardened. "I'm working on a self-portrait . . . a new and improved Gray."

"I'd like to see the picture when it's finished."

"Would you? Have you read Wilde's *Dorian Gray*?" A curious light shone in the artist's eyes.

"Wilde's story didn't end well for Dorian Gray," observed Castro.

Gray waved him off. "As they say, nothing ventured, nothing gained. Listen, our conversation about Gina before you left the set . . . I don't want you to think I don't miss her and mourn her."

Castro was still preoccupied with the other Gray. Why had the artist brought Wilde's story into the conversation?

"I meant it when I told you Gina was authentic," Gray

said quietly, as if strangers were present. "I'm glad the idomean's gone, though. There was something rather psychic about it." The artist patted his heart. "Gina once told me she was bound for the havens."

Castro started to respond, but Gray wasn't listening. "I was wheeling her past the library when she said that," Gray continued. "Maybe she had a premonition."

The artist hung his head, and Castro clumsily shook his scabby hand before leaving the room.

Castro went to the library, hoping to find solitude, to reflect on all he had heard and needed to do—and soon—but he wasn't alone in the room. Clement was looking out the window.

Approaching the rain-splattered pane, Castro had a view of the backs of set façades.

"You don't have to look hard to realize that none of this is real," observed Clement.

"The façades have held up," Castro responded.

"I wasn't talking about the buildings. Your news about Philby and the tunnel wasn't a big surprise. A while back, I was warned the Bureau was on the scent."

Castro wanted to press Clement, but the time wasn't right. "What's wrong with Sarah? She's hardly said a word to me."

"Why don't you ask her yourself? Maybe she doesn't want you to go down with the ship."

Castro heard a peal of thunder, followed by loud laughter from somewhere in the building. "Want to go fishing?" Clement asked him.

18

The Custodian

The rain had slackened by the time the two men reached the shoreline. Clement put a hand on Castro's shoulder and pointed to the pine-needle-strewn ground adjacent to the footpath. "Bear . . . our bear."

Staring at the irregularly shaped indentations in the sandy soil, Castro said, "How do you know?"

"I know bear tracks, and these are enormous."

Both were wearing wide-brimmed hats Clement had retrieved from his locker.

A ten-foot ribbon of brown sand sprinkled with mustard-colored plants lined much of the pond. Clement led Castro to a place along the beach about a hundred yards from where the path dead-ended at the shore.

"Mallard Lake is deeper here. Let's fish. But first, this."

Clement handed Castro a tube of insect repellent. "I always put this on when I'm in the woods. Mosquitos and flies can be a nuisance. You certainly don't want any hitch-hiking ticks."

Castro's mind was always working. If he had picked up a tick on his hike over the hill that first day, he surely would have known it.

The pond—or lake—was several hundred yards wide and about a quarter-mile long. The two stood side-by-side, rods in hand. Castro accepted a worm from Clement and baited his hook, watching the custodian cast before he tried himself, losing two worms before he had the hang of it.

The Red Cards' caretaker wasn't a handsome man, though his rough-textured features were memorable. Clement's shoulder-length hair lapped the collar of his blue denim shirt. Grief or worry seemed to have taken a toll on him since he and Castro had first met.

"Hardly anyone knows about this place," Clement whispered. "Natural lake with a stream feeding it over there." He pointed west. "A long time ago, someone built a rock dam at the outlet to raise the water level. When it's warm and I'm bothered and . . ."

". . . bewildered," Castro cut in.

"I sometimes strip down and have a paddle around the lake. Mind if I smoke?"

The writer said he didn't mind. Clement lit one up.

Castro caught the first fish, a small perch. Clement hooked the next three, a trio of bass. After a while, they sat in the sand with the sun emerging from behind the heavy clouds.

"I underestimated you," said Castro, feeling a jerk on his line and cranking hard.

"That makes two of us. He got your bait. Too much chatter."

Clement caught two more bass and two perch before Castro brought in his next fish. "What's the limit?" the writer asked, fumbling to unhook the fish.

"Whatever we can eat. We're not fishing for fun . . . well, not just for fun. I admit this is therapy for me."

Clement re-baited his hook and cast into the lake, describing an elegant arc with his line.

"What other animals do you see around here?" Castro asked him.

Clement jerked his rod. "Fox, muskrat, coyote, raccoon . . . deer, of course, lots of birds."

"Wolves?"

"I've heard they're around. Why do you ask?"

"I ran into some during filming."

Clement said, "The set's next to a million-acre preserve, so I wouldn't be surprised. Were you alone?"

"With Letta Lane, and to hear Letta tell it, the wolves were all my fault."

Castro was glad he had accepted Clement's invitation to come along. He could learn to like fishing, and it took his mind off the action he was contemplating.

In the meantime, he was still reflecting on his conversation with John Gray, especially the artist's oblique reference to Dorian Gray. Did John harbor the hope that he might achieve a transformation that wouldn't merely falsify his appearance or wash off as makeup did?

Clement jerked his line. "This was a popular place for the Algonquin, judging by the tools and arrowheads I've found along the shore."

The shaggy river birches up the shoreline were stirring, and the tips of the big pines on the wood line were gently swaying.

"Have you lived in these parts all your life?" Castro asked.

"Since my parents moved here from Detroit when I was ten."

"How did you get to the set?"

"Not the way you'd figure . . . damn, he got my bait." Clement brought in his line and put a fresh worm on the hook. "I dropped out of high school my senior year. Managed to settle down long enough to earn my mechanic's certificate. I read an ad for this job and thought it might be a good match. I didn't care much for company in those days. About that time, someone came to visit me—a welcome visit. I gave this person my standard tour of the set. That's when the question was sprung."

Who else could this person be except for the mysterious Producer J?

Clement made it sound so simple, but Castro knew better than that. "Some of the residents brought their own cars. Where are they now?" he asked.

"A junkyard in Harrisville reserves me a corner of their property. The cars are the least of our worries."

The man carefully set down his rod on the sand. "I have something to say to you, Hume. When you leave, talk Sarah into going with you. I know she likes you. That's why you came back, isn't it? Even if it doesn't work out with you two, she'll be gone when the SSB trample us."

"I'll try. Your job is to keep Max from trampling me."

In a half-whisper, Clement said, "The night you returned to the set, you suggested the SSB haven't trampled us yet because Philby is afraid of something."

"Or something's holding her back. She practically nailed me to the wall one night in L.A. By then, she knew about the tunnel, and she knew Red Cards were on the set."

"Maybe you're a high-profile trophy."

If Clement could see Castro's apartment, he would adopt a different view. Castro was reticent to speak about the connection between the SSB commander and Fiona. "There's something else, but I better not say any more. Not yet."

"We all have our secrets," the site manager admitted.

Of this Castro was certain: he couldn't count on Philby holding off forever, so he had to make his move first.

A blue heron passed overhead, rowing through the air before settling in the shallows on the other side of the lake.

Castro said, "I know Sarah's very sick, and I know someone who will treat her. Will you help me get her there?"

Clement was amazed. "Of course I will."

But Castro required more. "You told the residents they needn't worry about the chips that were implanted when they received their Red Cards. Perhaps the Trillium set is too remote for the SSB to locate them, but if I bring Sarah to Detroit—"

"Our location has nothing to do with those chips," Clement interrupted him. "At one time, the SSB could locate Red Cards in Antarctica if they wanted to."

"You disabled the chips?"

The custodian laughed. "I'm competent with a paintbrush and fishing pole, not with removing or disabling tracking chips. I told them not to worry about the chips, but I didn't tell them why." He smiled. "Ever heard of Lucas Paine?"

Castro's line had been out of the water for several minutes. "Who hasn't? They called him The Paine Monster. He murdered six people."

Clement finished landing a bluegill. "Fine story, that. The bigger the lie, the more people fall for it." He cast his line yet again. "You may recall Paine's was a restricted access trial. The Bureau asserted jurisdiction because they claimed one of their agents had been murdered by Paine. Did you know Lucas Paine had a Red Card because he had severe autism?"

Just when Castro thought he had figured this man out, something new emerged.

"You wouldn't have heard about Paine's Red Card in the news," Clement informed him. "Lucas Paine's actual crime was a back-door breach of the SSB chip network. He was a master lightning stealer—destroyed the software, preventing the Bureau from locating and tracking Red Cards. You see, Paine's autism didn't affect his genius, any more than a card affects John's art or Colleen's marathon walking.

"The Bureau's still scrambling to produce better software and chips. In the meantime, the SSB have other ways to locate Red Cards, but nothing as effective as those chips."

If all this was true, only Producer J could have been the source of this deep intelligence.

"Are you fishing for birds?" Clement grumbled good-naturedly.

"Sorry." The screenwriter reeled in his line.

"Let's go," Clement said, picking up his tackle box. "You're serious about getting Sarah treatment, aren't you? What do you want me to do?"

By the time the warehouse was in sight, the clouds had piled up again and more rain was surely on the way. Castro carried a basket of nine bass, seven perch, and a bluegill. He had a word for Clement before they joined the others. "The day we met, I asked if you lived alone, and you said you prefer it."

"That was before you discovered I don't live alone. I made the mistake of falling in love with someone I can never have."

Sarah and Fiona were waiting for them.

"Fish!" Fiona shouted.

19

Neverland

With a puzzled stare, Sarah sat up and moaned.

Castro could tell she was frightened and tried to reassure her. "Trust me. You need to get up and get dressed; wear these clothes."

He was as amped up as he had ever been, but at least he knew what was happening.

"Are the SSB here?" she asked, now wide-eyed.

"No, get dressed."

"These aren't my clothes," protested the woman.

Castro had never seen her like this. He steeled himself. "Dress, then sit in front of the mirror and close your eyes."

"These are your clothes."

When Castro didn't answer, Sarah passively acquiesced. "Turn your back."

A minute later, he heard her say, "All right, I'm dressed."

At the mirror, Castro sheared her hair with a scissors, followed by an electric razor. Sarah neither spoke nor moved When he had finished, she said, "Now that you've turned me into a boy—"

"Put on this hat and jacket."

He hoped that his crude barbering and Clement's bulky jacket would successfully hide her feminine features.

She looked in the mirror one more time and choked back a sob.

"I promise, it couldn't be helped."

Castro led her through the dark hallway to the rear exit, where he grabbed a small travel bag by the door. "When we get outside, we need to make a run for the woods," he said. Perhaps the shadow thing Colleen had seen was only a swooping owl or some such creature, but he wasn't taking any chances by tarrying in the open.

"Can you tell me where we're going?"

"If we're caught on the way, the less you know, the better. Let's go."

They trotted out the door, hand in hand. Castro kept them running until they reached the wood line. He stopped beneath a stand of pines where the two applied Clement's bug juice. "We'll be hiking for a while. Keep your eyes open."

"What do you expect to see?"

"Nothing, I hope."

She made him look at her. "Do you know where you're going? If you haven't noticed, it's starting to rain."

"Good, no moonlight."

Castro removed a pencil flashlight from his coat, directing the beam at the ground in front of them.

Sarah said, "We didn't bring anything. How long will we be gone?"

"Two days." He wouldn't reveal how perilous those two days would be. "I have supplies in the bag."

"The others will be frightened when—"

"Clement will talk to them later today." He had to keep her focused on the mission.

The stream bank was reedy. Wary as he was, Castro let the light play up and down the banks on both sides of the stream. Sarah didn't say a word.

"This way," said Castro, pretending to be resolute.

As it turned out, Clement and his canoe were just around the next bend in the stream.

"You look like one of those Neverland boys," Clement told Sarah. "Get in. We have a way to go, and we need to arrive before sunrise."

Castro sat in the rear of the canoe, Sarah in front, the custodian behind her.

"I'll let you know if you need to paddle," Clement said. "Otherwise, sit still and don't rock the boat."

Downstream they went at a glide. Fortunately, the rain had stopped, night birds began calling, and the emerging moon supplied enough light for them to see several hundred feet up and down the stream. Rills exited the woods on either side, some so placid they were almost invisible, some bubbling from elevated outcrops. The flies weren't as bad as Castro had feared, especially after they exited the stream into a river three times as wide.

Barely a hundred yards into the river, Clement whispered, "I'll be damned. There she is."

Castro's heart skipped a beat. Had Philby followed them, in spite of all the precautions they had taken? His eyes followed the line of Clement's finger to the far bank. There, in an opening between a cluster of tall cypress, stood the mammoth. It might have been watching them as its head was pointed in their direction, or else the beast had caught their scent. Even at night, enough light reflected off the water to illuminate the creature's shaggy coat and massive curved tusks.

"Look . . . behind her, a calf," Sarah whispered. "That means a herd, not just a solitaire."

For all their worry, the mammoth invigorated the trio, especially Sarah. Upon entering the river, Clement had picked up the rowing pace, calling on Castro and Sarah to help in stretches where the current slackened.

"Are we going to make it?" Castro asked.

"We'll make it."

"He'll wait, won't he?"

Clement nodded. "He'll wait, but I don't want anyone else waiting with him."

A glimmer of light shone to the east when the river exited the forest and its dense canopy. They passed open land and cultivated fields; early-riser lights glowed inside some of the farmhouses along the way.

Another half hour passed before they reached Lake Huron. A pilot boat was anchored about a hundred yards from shore, just south of the river effluence. Clement lost no time in making for it.

Under a thin haze, the still lake was opalescent, much like an Impressionist painting.

As they closed in on the boat, half the sun was already above the horizon. The man on deck, fair-haired and ruddy, first helped Castro and Sarah on board, then said to Clement, "You're not taking that *dinghy* back upstream, are you?"

"I am," the custodian replied.

"Good way to have a coronary. Park it at the dock and take my car. We can haul it back later."

"Nope."

"Be stubborn. Come up and have some coffee at least."

"You need to go, and so do I. And thank you." Clement was already turning the canoe around. A minute later, he was halfway back to shore.

The square-chinned captain took a good look at Castro and Sarah. "How was the trip?"

"We saw a mammoth and her calf on the riverbank," Sarah said.

"I'd ask if you're sure, but you couldn't mistake something that big. I'm Evan Masters. Now, you two get below. I'm sure you need sleep, and it wouldn't do to have you seen on deck so close to the river. You can come up later."

Castro was worn out, and he knew Sarah must be as exhausted as he was. Both climbed into bunks below deck. He wanted to comfort her, but what gave him that right? Moreover, this was far too early in the gambit for comfort —for either of them.

When Castro awoke, Masters was gently shaking his shoulder. Sarah's bunk was empty.

Castro shot upright.

"She's fine," the man assured him. "Up top getting some sun. I made coffee and sandwiches."

Sarah was sitting in a deck chair on the prow, having removed her jacket but still wearing Castro's cap. The boat was motoring at a good speed but not so fast as to produce turbulence on deck.

Still weary, Castro told himself a few hours' sleep was better than nothing.

Masters scanned the waterscape. "Sleeping speed. That's what my wife used to say. We'll speed up now. Sandwiches are on the table."

Castro walked forward until he was standing at Sarah's shoulder.

"The jacket stays on," Castro remarked.

To the boaters who passed them, these three men were enjoying an early autumn day on the water.

This expanse of water triggered Castro's fertile imagination. Why were people afraid of boneyards when lakes, forests, and roads were far more dangerous? Yes, dead bodies resided in cemeteries, but people actually died in lakes, oceans, and forests, and on roads, too. Castro was thinking about Letta—how they had almost come to a grisly end in the forest and how the ocean had finished her off. His parents and Cynthia, too, were killed on a road.

"What are you thinking about?" Sarah asked him.

"Forests, oceans, lakes."

"Pleasant thoughts. I envy you."

They had been cruising south for some time when Castro asked Masters, "How long until we arrive?"

"About an hour to the dock. Want me to call ahead for a cab?"

"We'll walk."

"I figured as much. Will you two join me . . . a cigar and a glass of Scotch? About the only place left where I can smoke in peace."

Masters' words reminded Castro of Starling, the reason he and Sarah were here.

"Just the cigar," said Castro.

"Just the Scotch," Sarah chimed in. "No cigars for me when the floor's moving."

As close to relaxed as he had felt in weeks, Castro said, "May I ask how Clement persuaded you to take us on?"

Masters veered to the right to give an approaching boat plenty of leeway. "He didn't have to twist my arm, if that's what you mean. I'll do anything to screw those pirates."

Masters lifted the glass of Scotch to his lips. "It all started with Helen's Red Card. We knew about Red Cards, never thought it would happen to us . . . to her. Helen grew despondent. I missed the signs.

"One day, I came home and found a note. That's the way she'd planned it, so I wouldn't be tied down. Helen wasn't crazy, but the Red Card threw her off balance, and she was worried about me. I had to call the SSB to confirm she was dead. The person who talked to me might have been describing a dead squirrel. Jeff did me a favor by recruiting me for this job."

Masters opened a box next to his chair and removed a pair of binoculars, training them on a circling bird. "Appears to be the genuine article," he said, "not an SSB sky hawk."

"What would you do if it was?" asked Castro.

"Shoot it down," Masters blustered, refilling his glass.

They passed Belle Isle and approached the Detroit pleasure craft dock, as anonymous a docking location as could be found in the city. Castro expected the SSB to be waiting for them, as he had expected them to intercept the canoe, or Masters' boat, but they docked without incident.

Masters helped them up to the dock. He didn't waste any time returning to the river.

Sarah offered Castro a wry smile. "I'll get my land legs in a minute. Then, off to Neverland, Peter Pan."

20

Red Card Underground Railroad

Approaching a city park, Castro said to Sarah, "It's time to tell you what we're up to."

She turned to him expectantly.

"When I was in L.A., I was given the name of a doctor on the Red Card Underground Railroad."

She stopped walking. He could hear her breathing. "Do you trust the person who gave you the card?"

The same question Gray had asked him. "When I was young, he was my hero. Ron Starling . . . *Shadow Time.*"

"You told Starling about all of us?"

"I didn't, but he knew something because he gave me this doctor's name." Castro handed the card to Sarah.

"Starling said the doctor would know we are legitimate by the card. The date and time were set by the person who answered the phone, along with instructions about where to go."

"This is scary," Sarah said. "You should have told me sooner."

"Maybe. If you want to go back, I won't object."

Sarah sighed. "I'll be all right."

The two sat side by side on a bench facing the hospital. The park had a limestone tholos in the center that housed a public lavatory. Although vagrants passed by, no one bothered them, perhaps because of the patrol car at one end of the park that made Castro nervous.

Vespulae two-wheelers made up much of the motor traffic on the road circling the park. A roar erupted whenever someone gunned his bike.

"Sitting and waiting is harder than our midnight adventure," Sarah said.

"I understand about the wait, but if something had gone wrong along the way and we'd arrived late, we might have missed the appointment."

Sarah wasn't listening to him because her gaze was fixed on a mother and her two children across the park. The trio had formed a triangle some twenty feet apart from each other. They were throwing an orange ball around, accompanied by shouts and laughter. The sturdy boy appeared to be about ten, and the younger girl possessed a willowy physique like her mother. Vagrants and those purposefully navigating the park gave the boisterous trio a wide berth.

For some minutes, Sarah watched them play, a broad smile on her face. The boy was adept at behind-the-back tosses that were almost as true as his overhand throws.

"They remind me of the Stewarts . . . the family I traveled with," Sarah observed. "The same uninhibited joy. Was your family like that?"

Castro thought for a moment. "Cynthia and I were always close. Our parents were attentive, but they kept us at arm's length. I have a few good memories of family outings."

"Just a few?" she asked, as the family trotted out of the park.

"I was fortunate. I realized that after I lost my parents."

"Are you nervous?" Sarah asked.

Though he had told himself he had to be a reassuring presence, he couldn't fool Sarah. "I don't like sitting in the open for so long," he said. "I don't like that prowl car over there. I'm paranoid about the SSB."

"You're doing a good job of pretending to be calm."

He took her hand. She didn't resist. "I wrote that into the script: *Castro Hume, feigning serenity, converses with Sarah.*"

This brought another smile to Sarah's face.

At almost suppertime, a short, pudgy man in jeans and a well-worn sweater approached them. At first, Castro thought he was another vagrant, but as he came closer, Castro recognized a determined expression on the man's face.

"A word with you," said the stranger.

A statement or a question? Castro's pulse was racing. If this man wasn't a vagrant, he must be a plainclothes policeman. Or worse, SSB.

"A little theater first for anyone watching us." The man scratched his rear end dramatically. "I'm Brother Gerry. I'm a friend of Dr. Weems. I'll be driving you to your lodgings after the meeting . . . a green Volksalux. A tight fit for three, but we don't have far to go. I'll meet you there," the man said, nodding to a street corner adjoining the park.

Could Castro trust this funny-looking character? Well, he had been living on trust since he had left the reptile world, so what was one more reckless move?

Gerry said, "Don't be in a hurry to go inside. Wait until dark, at least dusk. You know where you're going?"

Castro nodded.

"I shouldn't stay any longer. I'm known around here as a troublemaker—by the authorities, I mean, because I take up for these indigents. Act as if you belong in the hospital. Look as relaxed as you can, laugh now and then. I'll see you at the corner."

Gerry was halfway across the park when Sarah said, "I

can't believe I'm so tired and anxious. An expedition every year used to be my motto. I was fit enough to go anywhere." She laughed timidly. "Today was a spa day compared to a day inside the Megatheria Preserve."

Castro's vacant expression must have prompted her to explain. "The Chile preserve isn't well known. Only a few hundred megatheria are contained in a protected area."

"Like a zoo?" he asked her, scanning the park for the twentieth time.

"Yes, except natural barriers rather than fences or walls, across five thousand acres. The animals live as they would in the wild."

"I don't even know what a megatheria is," said Castro.

"A megatherium is bigger than a breadbox and smaller than a mammoth. A giant ground sloth, up to four tons, up to twenty feet tall, huge hind legs for standing and reaching tree branches . . . long tongue and prehensile lips ideal for branches and leaves."

Delighted to see Sarah's spirits lifted, he asked, "How long were you in the preserve?"

"A month, night and day, tent lodging . . . nasty snakes and wheat spiders, too."

The longer he could distract her from what they had to do that evening, the better. "How close did you come to the sloths?"

If Sarah guessed what he was up to, she didn't care. "One morning, I crawled out of the tent and saw a female mega munching on a tree a few yards away. She saw me but didn't move away. I didn't stir for an hour."

A man in nurse's garb strolled past their bench, quieting Sarah for a minute.

"Bringing megafauna back to the world had to cost

an unimaginable amount of money," she continued. "Dr. Greenberg isn't a crackpot. He once told me that much more than science was motivating those genetic experiments."

"And?"

"And that's all he'd tell me. In those days, I didn't particularly care what motivated the experiments. All I cared about was studying live specimens."

One of her hands was shaking. "You must be exhausted," he said.

"I'm too anxious to feel anything else. Just tell me what to do, and I'll do it."

"Eat this," he said, handing her a sandwich from his tote bag.

She complied and afterward asked, "How did you get your name?"

"My uncle was a Cuban rebel. The Havana government executed him. My mother honored him by giving me his name—Castro."

Another restless half hour passed. The park had emptied out. A lone vagrant searched through one trash container after another.

"Let's go," Castro said to Sarah when he couldn't wait any longer. "It's getting dark, and I need to do something besides pretending I'm relaxed and happy. Remember, you're a boy, and don't speak unless you have to."

Castro took a moment to compose himself. He couldn't help how he felt, he could only do what he intended to do, and that was give Sarah a chance with Dr. Weems. He had to stay focused on this mission and nothing else. For her sake, he must hide his fear.

What had Gina said to him that evening in the parlor? *One must face things as they are.* Just before she had called him

Sir Galahad, or perhaps called him to be more like that brave and noble knight.

The two crossed the street and passed through the hospital's sliding glass doors. Castro had been instructed to march past the entrance attendant as if he knew where he was going.

They took one of the elevators to the fifth floor and walked down two long corridors with after-hours illumination before they encountered anyone—an older Asian man in a lab coat and a younger man in a suit, the two engaged in an animated conversation.

Castro missed the office he was seeking and had to double back. He heard music coming from behind the door. Who would greet them?

They were admitted by a tall, dark-skinned man with earnest eyes and a shaved head who was probably in his late thirties.

Background music was playing. "Hume?" whispered the black man.

Castro handed the man the card Starling had given him. The man put it in his shirt pocket rather than returning it and then shut the door behind them.

In a louder voice, the man said, "Come in, Mr. Parker. I'm Dr. Weems. This must be your son. Sorry I couldn't see you sooner. I understand your son suffers from insomnia." The man dramatically shook his head as he said, "Does the music bother you?"

"It's fine," Castro returned, taking the cue.

"Close the door, please," said Dr. Weems. "Eliot, before you tell me about your sleeping problem, let me read the information you brought with you."

Sarah's eyes widened when Castro handed Weems folded pieces of paper from an inside pocket of his coat. Castro had asked Clement to help him acquire medical information about Sarah's cancer, and the custodian—or Producer J—had delivered in spades.

The doctor took several minutes reviewing the documents.

"I see." Dr. Weems paused. In such a low voice that Castro could barely make out with the music playing, Weems said, "Are you experiencing symptoms?"

"Yes," Sarah whispered, going on to describe them in the same low voice.

"How many hours a day do you sleep?" Weems said in his louder voice, then he whispered, "Intense?"

Castro said, "He only sleeps three or four hours a night." Sarah whispered, "Not yet, but worse than when I arrived at . . . where I live."

"You'll be sleeping at least eight hours a night when I'm finished with you, young man." In a barely audible voice, he said, "I'm going to give you a potent injection to trigger a massive immune system response and therapeutic meds to finish the treatment at home."

Castro spoke up. "He's been having trouble sleeping for a year," and in a lower voice, "Will it make him sick?"

Fortissimo: "I'm giving him a B-vitamin injection. When you return home, he can take one of these pills every third night before bed." *Sotto voce*: "No helping the side effects. It's powerful immunotherapy. As I won't see you again, we have to push the limits . . . all right?"

They were all pushing the limits: Sarah, Weems, Clement, Masters, even Starling, who was connected to this network of SSB defiers.

Sarah never hesitated. "Let's get on with it."

"Now, roll up your shirt sleeve," Weems said, in his normal voice. "Not so bad, was it, Eliot? The pills will help him sleep." He proceeded to speak behind his hand. "With the injection and the pills, she'll be bedridden for a few days and nauseous for another week or so."

Apparently, the Red Card Railroad recruited ventriloquists.

"Eliot, try not to stay up too late, and no soda or candy before bed." Weems said softly, "These therapies are passed down the railroad, so somewhat higher risk."

"What makes you think the treatment will work?" asked Sarah.

The man nodded, and whispered, "This medicine isn't available to people like us. Suffice it to say if this medicine works the way it's supposed to, you may experience full remission." In his theatric voice, Weems added, "Don't take a pill in the car, Eliot. Wait till you're home."

"Thank you, Doctor."

Weems gave her a big grin. "My pleasure, young man. Can you find your way out?"

Castro took Weems' hand and gripped it hard, feeling a powerful squeeze in return.

"How do you know the person who sent us here?" Castro whispered.

Weems remained silent for so long that Castro already had a hand on the doorknob when the doctor replied in a surprisingly clear voice.

"Ancient pines live on mountaintops where nothing else can long survive. Their wood is extremely dense and resinous to resist pests and predators."

Had Weems misunderstood Castro's question?

"Some hang on to life by a fibrous thread. I have visited several specimens on high mountains . . . and attended to one in the heart of the Cosmopolis."

The pair didn't say a word to each other until they were outside the hospital, when Sarah said, "He knows or suspects the authorities are listening to him. The music makes eavesdropping harder for them. He can't lack for patients and opportunities. Why does he do it?"

A question Castro had been asking himself since he lied to Philby and her agents on the set. "Why do Clement and Masters and Starling do it? To help and to hinder. Now, *young man*, let's see if we can find Gerry and get you settled before Weems' injection starts to take effect."

Empty of life, the park might have been a boneyard but for the absence of headstones. A tiny car was parked on the corner Gerry had identified. As the two approached, the Volksalux's lights flashed several times.

Opening the passenger door, Castro asked, "Where's the back seat?"

"I told you it'd be tight," said the anonymous driver.

"This isn't tight, it's a sardine can."

Gerry snorted. "A Leviathan isn't a luxury we can afford. Be happy I didn't bring our Vespula. You can walk if you prefer, but I wouldn't recommend it this time of night unless you're in good running shape . . . I mean *very* good."

"Is this a trick to get me to sit on your lap?" Sarah whispered to Castro.

"Here we go," said Gerry. "No necking, or you might tip this bug over."

"Where are we going?" Sarah asked their driver.

"We call it the Solanus Resort and Spa. All our residents have Red Cards or are well on their way to earning one."

"Who's Solanus?" said Sarah.

"Years ago, Brother Solanus was our doorkeeper. In those days, he convinced several of the SSB to join the Order."

In his muddled state, Castro spoke without thinking. "Don't you mean infiltrate the order?"

"Not in my case," Gerry answered.

When what their driver said had sunk in, Castro's heart skipped several beats.

"Hopefully, no SSB visits to our humble abode tonight. If they show up, keep quiet and pretend to be asleep. I can't keep them out, only warn our lodgers off listening to them."

Castro was confused. "Why would your people listen to the SSB?"

"Because those villains promise a week of feasting, all the booze and dope any addict could want. After that, who'd want to go back to the street? Why not send a termino-sapiensis check to Mom or little sister and go through the red door? The SSB has a quota, just like insurance salesmen. Last week, Henry took them up on their offer."

Castro said, "It's their choice, isn't it?"

Gerry grunted. "Almost missed my turn . . . Choice? Like offering fish to a cat. As you can see, I'm no lightweight . . . more Friar Tuck than Francis of Assisi. The SSB sends me caramel cake every month, their way of telling me who's in control."

"What do you do with the cake?" Sarah asked him.

"I eat it, of course. I told you, I'm no Francis. Here we are."

Gerry informed them that the old building had once been a sausage factory. Now, it was filled with cots occupied by his vagrants. Looking up, Castro saw that many of the ceiling tiles were missing. When he looked down, he saw the concrete floor was cracked and pitted.

Gerry said, "We've discounted the rates, just for you."

From the next bed, Castro heard Sarah whisper, "I'm afraid of dying."

He needed a few seconds to realize she was talking to Gerry, not to him.

"Before you leave, I'll take you to Solanus' tomb. You can talk to him about what's troubling you."

Another boneyard! This time, a real one.

Castro expected Sarah to object to Gerry's preposterous suggestion, but she didn't say another word.

21

White Cards

Castro heard loud retching.

Sarah's cot was empty.

He noticed Gerry's cot was empty, too.

Several of the residents were sitting up, rubbing their eyes, or stretching. Castro pulled the blanket up to his chin and took a series of deep breaths. Another long day beckoned.

Sarah returned on Gerry's arm, wan and shaky. "Maybe we should wait another day," Castro suggested.

"According to the doctor, one day won't make a difference," Sarah labored to say. "And every day we spend here could bring trouble down on these people. The sooner we're off, the sooner we'll be home."

In spite of how bad she felt, Sarah accompanied Gerry to the tomb. When she returned, she told Castro, "I'm ready now."

Castro pulled Gerry aside as Sarah gathered her things and said, "Why rub her face in death?"

"You could say a cocoon is the death of the creeping caterpillar."

Castro imagined the look Cooperwasser would give him if he tried a line like that.

Gerry drove them to the bus depot in a steady rain. Clouds seemed to perch on the roof of the tiny car. As gloomy as the weather was, Castro knew that for their purposes rain was better than bright sun, but that hardly lifted his spirits.

"These damn wipers," Gerry grumbled. "Solanus introduced me to the Logos and the power of speaking truth. Ever since I met you, I've been itching to reveal a secret."

The Volksalux skidded to a stop at a red light Gerry had almost missed. He had to back up the car to clear the intersection.

"When I was with the SSB, my job was surveillance. Not gumshoe stalking, collecting and analyzing data." His voice suddenly doleful, Gerry said, "I maintained what we called caviar maps, crowded with black dots where the Bureau herded Red Cards who resisted terminosapiensis."

How could Castro help wondering if Dana Philby kept a caviar map for the set?

"My job meant I was around the bosses. As it happened, the gauleiter himself was engaged in a highly classified operation involving a senator who'd been antagonizing the Bureau. One day, he forgot to deactivate his voice recorder after talking to the man."

The light changed and off they went.

"It was after midnight. I was alone in the data room when I overheard the gauleiter's conversation with someone—a long and serious conversation."

A car cut them off. Brother Gerry laid on the horn.

He continued speaking as if nothing had happened. "What I heard was that every terminosapiensized Red Card's organs and body parts are at the disposal of those who'd been awarded White Cards—to enhance and extend White Cards' lives. Also, some medicines are only available to White Cards."

Now, Gerry had Castro's full attention. Hadn't Ron Starling made a vague remark about White Cards?

Gerry went on. "That cheeky gauleiter called all of this red helotry. When you see how hard they pursue my people, isn't it easier to believe they do it for self-enrichment?"

"Physically speaking, your people are damaged goods," Castro observed.

"You may say so. This car isn't much to look at, but you'd be surprised at how an expert could pick it apart for a smart profit. The engine and transmission have seen their best days, yet the tires and radio have a market."

The Volksalux pulled up to the curb in front of the bus station. Gerry said, "Make of that information what you will. Send the news up and down the railroad if you can, but before you go let me offer a morsel of encouragement. When one rejects humility, he loses the ability to see the truth about himself. Our enemies take reckless risks because they think they're invincible. Listen to me, both of you! Those having many resources rely on them. Those having none must learn resourcefulness.

"Shortly after I left the Bureau and came to Detroit, I told our humble doorkeeper about the SSB harvesting body parts. My news brought tears to his eyes. I shall never forget what he said: 'Those human harvesters—Blessed be *man* in all his designs . . . yet, it is also said that the man who waits for a dead man's shoes is in danger of going barefoot.' "

Sarah hadn't needed Gerry's bucket on the way, but when they arrived at the depot, she bolted into the lavatory.

Gerry grabbed Castro's arm and whispered, "Take care of her."

When Sarah finally returned, Castro shook off his many worries and said, "I have our tickets. We're leaving soon. Sit down before you keel over."

Seated on a bench, Sarah put her head on his shoulder. "Why aren't we returning the way we came?" she murmured.

"Clement and I decided to switch things up."

"Don't you expect them to be watching the set? Oh, oh, I'll be back." She jerked to her feet. "Don't let the bus leave without me."

With her every trip to the lavatory, Castro's heart sank. Soon, Sarah's pretty blue eyes were a mess, streaked with purple strands, and her face was swollen.

She clutched Castro's arm all the way to their seats. Though he was famished, he was resolved to consume nothing in her presence.

Scanning the seven other people on the bus, Castro was confident that none of them was Philby, but he couldn't rule out an SSB agent or two among them: a middle-aged man wearing a fedora; a couple who might be in their forties; a young man with a crew cut and tattoos on both arms; a corporal in uniform; an old man wearing a coat and tie; and a teenage boy all by himself.

Castro broke out in a big smile as he imagined the hatted man's third eye concealed beneath his fedora and the corporal's third arm hidden beneath his jacket.

"What's so funny?" Sarah managed to say.

"*Will the Alien Please Raise His Hand*?"

"Are you losing your mind?"

"Not every *Shadow Time* episode was dark or creepy. I promise that episode was hilarious."

The memory of that episode had made him happy for a moment—no small thing.

Rain pelted the bus. After Sarah's second trip to the toilet in fifteen minutes, she fell back into her seat. "Take my word for it, a bus with a toilet that hasn't been cleaned in days is the last place you want to get sick in. If I don't die of cancer, I'm likely to perish from the plague. Do you think we're being followed?" she asked him in a whisper.

"We did everything we could, so did Clement, Masters, Dr. Weems, and Gerry."

"All of you have taken big risks for me. Don't think I don't appreciate it. Thank you, Castro."

"Two people shorten the road. The state hasn't put everyone under its boot yet . . . Now I sound like Starling."

For long stretches of time, Sarah sat with her eyes closed and head lowered. Though the bus wasn't warm, she was flushed and perspiring. Now and then, she panted.

Castro's stomach hurt and his head throbbed in sympathy with her suffering.

While in Los Angeles, Castro had tried to convince himself that extracting Sarah from the set was an act of mercy, but every time he had thought about her a raft of feelings were stirred—pity for all she had lost, anger at her persecutors, and something else that a man of words found hard to describe. Of course, he had written characters who were in love, but he had never imagined love could encompass such exhilaration and desolation.

He glanced at Sarah. Her eyes were open. Her lips were clenched.

If Dr. Weems' medicine cured Sarah, how could she be prevented from living a normal life? Or did White Cards mean that Sarah's recovery wouldn't matter to the Bureau?

The pained look Castro had come to recognize was on Sarah's face again, but after a minute, she rallied and said, "What's it like to meet your hero?"

"I talked to Starling for a few minutes when I was a boy. Even then, I recognized he wasn't the man I'd put on a pedestal. That didn't discourage me from following in his footsteps."

He put his arm around her. "I know you feel awful. I'm

still glad we saw Dr. Weems, and I'm glad he gave you the injection and the medicine."

She mopped her forehead with a wet paper towel. "I'll reserve judgment until being dead isn't more attractive than how I've felt since 2 A.M. I want to stay alive . . . for Fiona. She needs someone now that Gina's gone."

"I want you to stay alive for *me*," said Castro, causing Sarah's chalky face to turn pink. "Is it time to take your pill?"

"Sadist! We're almost to Tawas. I need to know how to prepare."

Castro hesitated. "A car's meeting us there. Another friend of Clement's."

Tawas City was cloudy, the rain having subsided to a drizzle. Castro and Sarah were the last to disembark. All the others had found transportation or gone inside the depot when the two finally stepped off the bus.

"Need to use the lavatory?" he asked her.

"I think I'm okay."

"You're not hungry, are you?"

A prolonged head shaking gave him his answer. "Go inside and get yourself something," she said.

"I can wait. There's the Morris."

The long-haired, long-bearded man driving the gray and salmon two-tone car didn't say a word to them all the way to the outskirts of Harrisville, where he pulled off the road and took a narrow dirt trail back to a red barn. A woman with hair longer than their driver's opened the barn door, and the man drove in, parking the Morris next to a familiar green truck.

The truck window was down. Clement said, "Get in the back. Down on the floor, under the burlap."

Opening the rear door of the custodian's truck, Castro noticed that the seats had been removed. He and Sarah did as Clement had instructed, as the man expressed a few words of gratitude to their driver.

Once the truck was moving, Clement asked, "How are you, Sarah?"

Castro was uncomfortably curled up on the floorboard with just his head outside the burlap, so he could only imagine how Sarah felt. "Don't waste any time getting back," Castro called out. "And no big waves if you can help it."

Clement said, "Masters hasn't been harassed. That's a good sign. Where did you bunk last night?"

"Indigent shelter. More Red Cards." Castro heard Sarah moan, and he said, "If I say stop, stop, and don't ask any questions."

Clement cleared his throat. "I have news, and you're not gonna' like it. John left us a note. He's gone. Don't ask me how, but he found an ad for a clinic in Chicago that cures diseases like his, a place Red Cards are encouraged to enlist."

"No . . . No," Sarah cried.

"Yes, he fell for it. That means Philby's playing cat and mouse with us."

Castro shifted position to relieve a stabbing pain in his hip. "The man who runs the shelter in Detroit told us the SSB use tricks like that on his people."

Clement slapped the steering wheel. "First Max, now John. All the precautions we took for your trip to Detroit, and that fool goes off to Chicago."

Starling had disputed the Gianni Grigio suicide story, had insisted that Grigio was a hero who loved his son, but Gray's strange behavior the last time he and Castro had met—the handsome father reference, the forced levity, the self-portrait connection to Dorian Gray—suggested the *idée fixe* of a cure for neurofibromatosis had already taken hold of the artist.

"Have you heard anything from Johnny?" asked Sarah.

"Not a word."

"When did he leave?" Castro asked.

"He was gone when I returned to the set."

"Where would Gray have gotten such an ad?" Castro wondered out loud. "Did you see it?"

"I saw it. Stashed inside his dressing table. Slick."

Sarah said, "I refuse to believe one of us is helping the SSB . . . stop the truck, please!"

The two men nervously waited while Sarah heaved behind the truck.

Moving down the road again, Clement said, "I was warned about an SSB project called Specter . . . fetuses altered in the womb, trained as children for stealth missions, human tree squirrels. The notion that the SSB is doing this to protect the state doesn't make sense. Protecting it from what? From sick and old people who are too busy getting through the day to cause anyone trouble?"

"Who told you this?" Sarah demanded.

"I can't tell you that."

Castro could—Producer J. He related what Gerry had told them about White Cards.

Clement cursed. "How could they keep such a thing secret?"

A passing vehicle sounded its horn.

"My fault—distracted motoring," the custodian said. "How could they keep it secret?"

Castro had been trying to connect the dots for days. "That might explain Dana Philby's obsession with renegade Red Cards, if she's obsessed with obtaining a White Card."

The writer reached over and patted Sarah's burlap. "We're going to get you home safe and sound."

"And then what?" she asked him.

And then what, he asked himself.

22

Another Philby

"Come for breakfast."

Fiona was standing next to Castro's bed with a nervous look on her face.

"Bad dream," he said with a grimace. "I'll join you in a minute."

A gigantic bear, Sarah's panic-laden treatment mission, Gray lured away, Philby lurking—no wonder he was having nightmares.

After breakfast, Castro invited Sarah to join him in the parlor. They brought their coffee with them. Sarah sat in front of him on the rug. The two false parlor windows depicted a bright sun with fluffy clouds, a carefree day.

They had been back almost a week, and Sarah seemed to be improving more quickly than the doctor had suggested. Though she wasn't yet eating full meals, she had an appetite again. She wore Colleen's purple scarf around her bare head, not because of the therapy but because Castro had made such a mess with the scissors and razor.

The first few days Castro and Sarah were back, John Gray had been a frequent topic of conversation, but with no word from the artist, the residents and Clement now avoided the subject because of what it portended for Gray, and for them, too.

Clement had revealed just enough about what had transpired when Sarah and Castro were away from the set to give the rest hope about Sarah's condition.

Colleen was impressed with Castro. "You pulled a fast one on those louses. When I met you, I thought you were a man of words, not action."

"I'm a man of words pressed into action," Castro had responded.

Fiona walked into the room and sat next to Sarah on the rug. "I have a surprise . . . guess."

"Jeff is catching fish," Sarah said.

The girl shook her head and clapped her hands. "We're going to see a photoplay tonight. Colleen says so."

Castro didn't have to guess which photoplay Fiona was talking about.

"Colleen's going to make popcorn," Fiona said, leaping to her feet and bolting out of the room.

Castro and Sarah shared a smile.

"Do you know Fiona's last name and how she found her way here?" Castro asked her.

"Fiona *Styles*. Gina brought her. They both lived in the Boston area. Fiona had a Red Card, of course. She was living in a Red Card facility. Gina said the place was pitiful. One night, a courageous room warden led Fiona to the delivery door where Gina was waiting with a friend who drove them to the train station. That very night, Gina and Fiona took an express to Pittsburgh. The conductor had herded them into a livestock car with a few benches for Red Cards. A stroke of fortune, as Gina put it, because inside a passenger car they would have stood out like penguins in a desert."

"Sixty-seven chickens, thirteen rabbits, and three pigs" Castro remarked, to Sarah's surprise.

"Jeff met them in Pittsburgh, sufficiently distant from

this hideaway, and drove them here—less than twenty-four hours from the Red Card facility in Boston to the set."

"How did those two ever manage?" Castro mused out loud.

Sarah nodded vigorously. "Gina may have been confined to that chair, but she was as sharp as a tack—she had to be to have survived for so long. She told me one can do wonders when risk doesn't matter."

Indeed, as Castro himself had experienced with Sarah in Detroit.

"One more thing," Sarah said. "You've seen Fiona helping in the garden and about the set. Gina's plan wouldn't have succeeded without Fiona's help. Once that young woman sets her mind to something, she's dauntless.

"Fiona loved Gina. That's why she followed Gina to her bedroom every night and helped her prepare for sleep."

Why Fiona had been waiting at Gina's door the night Sir Galahad wheeled the crippled damsel to her room.

"Do you know if Styles is Fiona's birth name?"

Sarah shook her head. "I assumed that's always been her name."

Castro said, "The night I left the set, I found a birth certificate someone had stashed in my bag for an infant by the name of Phiona—with a p-h—Philby, born in Boston."

Sarah's eyes widened. "Fiona's related to Dana Philby?"

"Why else would Gina—who else could it have been?—have put that information in my bag? Gina must have acquired the birth certificate before the two left Boston. After Philby came to the set, Gina must have figured out the connection. Don't ask me why Gina passed on that information to me."

Sarah didn't hesitate. "Because she knew you're capable of a lot more than you think you are. If Gina knew about this connection, Philby must know it, too. I can't believe she'd let her own—"

"Sister? That's my guess."

"I can't believe she'd let her sister live in the conditions Gina described, and then hunt her down when Fi had a chance at a decent life."

"You'd never do such a thing, so you can't believe someone else would. Philby asked me about Gianni Grigio when she barged in with her two brightlings. She guessed I'd make the connection between Grigio and Gray, a smokescreen to hide the real target—her sister."

"Why would the SSB let a trisomy 21 child live?" Sarah asked.

"For useful body parts—Gerry's Volksalux story. In Philby's case, maybe more than that." He saw her perplexed expression and went on. "Bear with me. Gina Miller, a Red Card from Boston, was known to be devoted to *Stars Too Bright.* Fiona also resided in Boston and went off the grid about the same time as Gina. With that information, it wouldn't have been hard for Philby to establish the identity of a disfigured woman in a wheelchair who knew Fiona.

"I then traveled cross-country to the Trillium set. What could an Oscar-winning screenwriter be up to on an empty set? Philby had believed that Fiona Styles and Dana Philby were permanently separated, all documentation destroyed years ago. Suddenly, Fiona Styles vanishes. Who assisted her and why? To Philby, someone going to all that trouble for a trisomy 21 Red Card was inconceivable without an ulterior motive."

"What motive could Philby have suspected?" prodded Sarah.

"Haven't you guessed? Someone seeking to destroy Dana Philby by connecting her to Fiona Styles. That's what the

SSB commander feared. When the connection between Fiona, Gina, this site, and Castro Hume came to light, Dana Philby had to act. But cautiously. She couldn't risk the sibling connection being revealed. She first had to learn who knew what, so she could deal with everyone who posed a risk."

"They'll have to kill me before I let them hurt Fi!" Sarah flamed.

He hadn't intended to upset Sarah, but he had wanted her to know what he knew about Fiona. Now, Castro hoped to shift the conversation. "Fiona runs her finger over book spines in the library and over nameplates on the actors' room doors. What's she doing?"

But Sarah's worried look persisted. "It's a game Fi plays. She counts the letters . . . Do you ever think about your sister?"

Castro's inner eye zoomed to the memory of Cynthia in the back yard the day before everything went to hell.

"I'm sorry," she quickly said. "Of course, you do."

The warehouse loudspeaker interrupted them, Clement announcing that a busload of visitors would be arriving soon.

"Listen, Sarah. I want to ask you something. Please hear me out. I'd like you to come with me to L.A."

Unintentionally, he'd magnified her distress. "What are you asking me?"

"I'm not suggesting you move in with me."

"Did Jeff ask you to do this?"

"I was going to anyway."

She nodded. "Thanks for being honest."

"I want you to come with me, Sarah."

Tears welled in her eyes. "You barely know me. Who knows if I'm really cured? Where would I live?"

"The story editor for *Stars* teaches at UCLA. She told me you could stay with her until we figure something out."

"You have a devious mind. You know how much I'd love to be back at a university. Don't have any illusions that I'm a wealthy woman. With my illness and Red Card, I'm practically destitute."

"So am I."

"You don't paint a very attractive picture. You have to give me time to think."

"I know it's a big decision. When you consider it, I want you to know how I feel about you."

"We should go," Sarah said. "The visitors will be here soon. Jeff has asked us to go into the tunnel from now on."

"Now that the SSB know about the tunnel, it isn't a refuge anymore—it's a trap," Castro objected.

"Ask Max if the tunnel has ever been a refuge. Going up and down is especially hard on him."

Fiona and Last were already in the tunnel when Castro and Sarah arrived at the open hatch. The rug had been rolled up, and as Sarah started down, Colleen and Clement joined them.

"Get a move on," Clement groused. "They're almost here."

Castro went down last. Clement closed the hatch over the ladder. Castro didn't know why he was surprised at the condition of the tunnel, as Cooperwasser wouldn't have wasted money on bells and whistles for a parlor trick. Still, what awaited him when he reached the bottom was a sand floor, cracked walls, and a ceiling that was barely six feet high—Cooperwasser was only five and a half feet tall. Fortunately, none of the residents was over six feet, but the low ceiling gave Castro a claustrophobic feeling.

The tunnel was illuminated by bare bulbs attached to the

walls, serviced by electric wire tacked to the concrete. The air in the unventilated space was stale and heavy.

Last was breathing hard and blocking the entire runway. "I'm not coming down here every time Jeff gets a flea up his ass," muttered the big man.

Colleen said to Sarah, "That scarf looks lovely on you, dear. And it will look even nicer with my silver pin."

Time crept in that confined, gloomy space. A saddening silence descended on the group. Even Last clammed up, closed his eyes, and rested his head against the concrete wall.

At one point, Castro noticed that Colleen had wandered deeper into the tunnel, now a frail-looking gray shape in the dim light.

He joined her but kept silent, and for some time she didn't say anything, either.

Suddenly, Colleen erupted with a torrent of words. "I never spoke to anyone like I spoke to you the night you returned from California. As if you weren't burdened enough."

He took her bony hand. That September night, Colleen had come alive to him.

Maybe she saw this in his expression, because the old woman said, "I'm sorry for dragging you around the set that night. At ninety-three, having to hide from monsters, who knows if I'll ever have another chance to say what I want to say.

"Perhaps you guessed that not all Johnny's art was cheerful. We're a mixture of colors and shade. Johnny knew that."

Where had all this come from? Was the devil-may-care old woman he had gotten to know just a performance?

He thought she was finished until she said, "Do you think there are unblemished colors somewhere?"

"Gina thought so."

Tears streamed from Colleen's eyes. "Gina did think so. Thank you for reminding me."

Castro thought he heard something from the hatch end of the tunnel. His heart leapt. The others were looking up.

When the hatch finally opened, Clement invited them to return to the warehouse.

"How many visitors?" Last asked the custodian from down below.

"Seven."

"SSB?"

"Who knows? I don't think so. Two couples, two old women," Clement said, "and a midget."

"A midget!" Fiona exclaimed.

Up the ladder they came, one by one. After they'd all ascended, Fiona asked, "When are we going to see the photoplay?"

"That was supposed to be a surprise," Colleen remonstrated. "We're viewing *Stars Too Bright*, Castro, and we expect you to provide lively commentary."

Before they split up, Last pigeonholed Clement. By the look on their faces, whatever the two said to each other wasn't pleasant.

After a lackluster dinner prepared by Sarah and Castro, the six assembled in the library set, where a TV had been installed by the custodian. Colleen brought in three bowls of popcorn.

Early on, Sarah asked a question about Kenny Marks, who had portrayed young Oscar, and whose character was killed in the war.

Pausing the film, Castro said, "Ray Bolger had been pestering Cooperwasser to give him a serious part, but when the time came, Bolger had the opportunity to dance his way through a kids' story and turned us down. Bergin said, 'Once a hoofer, always a hoofer.' So, Cooperwasser offered the part to Marks."

"Another story, please," Colleen eagerly requested.

Too eagerly, Castro thought. Since they'd emerged from the tunnel, Colleen might just as well have been the pugnacious old woman he'd met that first night on the set.

Castro plumbed his memory, seeking something he dared to reveal. "For a late addition scene, the carpenters and electricians had to trick out the north side of the warehouse for the Drake's masked ball—an outdoor scene featuring dozens of delicate Chinese lanterns moved indoors because Cooperwasser wouldn't trust this scene to the wild world. Inside the warehouse, he could tincture his man-made sky with dozens of bright stars and an especially red Mars. Try to imagine—"

The site alarm blared, bringing Clement to his feet. "Stay here. Clean everything up and shut everything down. Be ready to go into the tunnel," he barked, walking briskly out of the room.

"No sense wasting perfectly good popcorn," Colleen said after Clement had gone.

"I'm not going down again," Last insisted.

Because they were in a room with a live window, Colleen turned off both lamps, darkening the space.

"What was Kenny Marks like?" Sarah asked Castro.

Perhaps she was trying to calm Last and the others. Castro kept his voice low. "Marks was in a hurry from the day he arrived on the set. He hated this place and—"

Into that darkened room came two figures, Clement recognizable by his gait, the other child-sized.

"Turn on the lights," Clement said.

Standing next to the custodian was a well-dressed man, about three and a half feet tall, clean-shaven, with dark oval eyes and full lips.

"What the hell's this?" Last asked.

"*This* is Pedro Martinez," the little person snapped.

Clement said, "He was one of today's visitors. He drove back to the set. He has a letter from a person who vouches for him . . . a person I trust."

"How do you know the person you trust wrote the letter?" Castro asked, his eyes trained on Pedro.

"I'll produce my Red Card if that will alleviate your fears," Pedro said. "Mind if I have some popcorn? I missed supper tonight." The little man didn't wait for approval, lunging at the nearest bowl.

The letter in Clement's glove box had suggested Producer J might be under surveillance, so why would that person send another Red Card to the set?

"How did you find out about us?" Sarah questioned the new arrival.

Pedro gave Sarah a good looking over. "I'm a carnie. I travel year round. You'd be surprised at the people we meet on the road, the things we learn. Someone put me in touch with someone else who knows this set-up like the back of his hand."

Sarah wasn't satisfied. "This person must have informed you this is no resort, so why are you here?"

Pedro didn't hesitate. "Same reason I joined the circus —freedom. I'm used to doing for myself, so I won't be a burden. I might be useful."

"You'd have more freedom with the circus than you'll have here," Sarah responded, as if she were quizzing a student.

"That depends on your definition of freedom, sister. No matter where the circus goes, those spooks can always find me."

"Can you do tricks?" asked Fiona.

Pedro bowed from the waist. "Certainly, my dear."

23

A Boy's Life

With his head on the pillow, looking up at the struts and panels that made up the roof of the warehouse, Castro wasn't thinking about Pedro or Dana Philby because he was about to embark on the *memory express*, precipitated by Sarah's question about his sister.

Over the years, Castro had come to realize that his memory was vastly superior to that of others', rich in detail for events that had occurred years, even decades, earlier. He had also come to realize this talent was both a blessing and a curse because the bad memories he retrieved were as vivid as the good ones. In solitude and silence, he could close his eyes and retrieve past experiences with remarkable clarity, a process he had taken to calling the memory express—flippantly at first.

First, the boy and the girl in the Detroit park, then Sarah's question about Cynthia: "Do you ever think about your sister?" With each passing year, hadn't Cynthia been slipping away from him? Replaced by what—Scarlet, mountains of words, that Hollywood viper pit?

What he'd forgotten about the memory express—or didn't want to consider—was how capricious the experience could be. Would the express take him to the memory destination he desired?

It did not, but by then it was too late. The boy Castro was sitting at his bedroom desk composing a story, his lamp on as it was raining, Ron Starling's signed script and cigarette butt like holy relics on the desktop.

A heavy knock on the door—not his bedroom door, the front door of the house—wrenched him away from the story. Hoping the visitor would go away, the boy tried to reapply himself to the scene he was composing.

"You have to answer," the memory express Castro said to the boy. "They're not going away."

The boy got up from his chair, threw his pen across the room, and dashed to the front door, trying to keep the next sentence of the story intact in his mind.

The knocking was growing louder, like Mr. Death's impatient knocking at the old woman's door in Starling's *Visitor in the Dark.* The boy had a sinking feeling—no, that was the *express* Castro, who knew what was on the other side of the door. The boy was barely thinking about the caller.

The express Castro followed the boy out of the room and down the hall into the over-furnished living room with floral print wallpaper and copious trinkets and novelties.

His Aunt Miranda was outside staring at the boy through the glass, waving to him in a spooky way.

The express Castro saw the spot on the carpet where his father had spilled coffee on the way out of the house that morning. His parents had been in a hurry. They had been on their way to the lake, but they had to drive Castro to the *Shadow Time* fan convention Ron Starling was attending before they could leave town.

The boy pulled open the door. His Aunt Miranda and Uncle Pat were holding hands, something the boy had never witnessed before. That day, Miranda was wearing a green and white dress. As always, her makeup was impeccable. Pat wore an open-collared dress shirt, blue slacks, and brown oxfords. Beneath the covered porch, the man held an umbrella over the pair.

Leaving the umbrella outside, Pat and Miranda pushed past the boy and slammed the door. The two adults stood in the foyer looking at each other.

"Go ahead and tell him," the express Castro said to Pat.

In spite of the umbrella, both were wet. Nevertheless, Miranda's makeup was perfectly intact.

"Your mother and father . . . and Cynthia were killed in a car smash," Pat said emotionlessly.

Naturally, the boy didn't believe them. The pounding rain made that compact room feel even smaller.

"A bad smash."

"They're at the lake," the boy protested. "He's a good driver."

"They're dead, Castro," said Miranda.

"They're not," the panicked boy insisted.

"Pack some things. You have to come with us," Miranda told him.

"I'm writing a story. Why are you lying to me?"

Thunder rocked the room.

From there, the express Castro was transported to his aunt and uncle's house, where the boy lay in an unfamiliar guest room bed—though quite familiar to the express Castro who had lived in this room for six years, until he went off to college and never returned.

Even after the boy moved in, the room had continued to double as a guest room, meaning he had to sleep on an air mattress in the basement when his aunt and uncle had overnight guests. That meant he couldn't keep his bookcase and desk because the room was too small to accommodate his furniture and guests.

That first night, with the lights out, the boy could hear every word his aunt and uncle said.

"What are we going to do?" his aunt asked her husband. "We don't know anything about raising children. And think of the cost."

The express Castro was paying attention because he knew what was coming.

Pat said, "We'll sell the house and furniture. That'll help."

"I can't believe they're dead. We just saw them yesterday."

After a lull in the conversation, Miranda said, "She didn't want him to go to that damn convention. They wanted to leave early, before traffic got heavy and the rain came, but he insisted. If they'd left when she wanted to leave, this wouldn't have happened."

No avoiding Miranda's words by either Castro, the boy experiencing the wound raw and stinging, the man as a numbing sadness that would never go away.

"Shh, he might hear you."

Miranda raised her voice. "Maybe he ought to hear. If he hadn't made them wait—"

"He's not too much trouble, to hear them talk."

"All kids are trouble. If we'd wanted kids, we'd have had our own."

"You've told me a million times you didn't want kids," whined Pat.

"And now you've got one," Miranda said. "I hope you're happy."

"The police said she had twelve toes," Pat remarked. "Imagine that."

His uncle's observation took Castro back to his own house and room, on an earlier night when all was still and his parents were safe in their own bed. Cynthia was on the other side of the wall, head to head with him. The boy was on the verge of sleep when he heard her familiar tapping, prompting him to kneel on the bed and remove the *Shadow Time* poster that had been tacked above the headboard. Behind this poster was a half-inch hole covered by another poster on Cynthia's side.

"You awake?" his sister's voice said.

"Yah." Even the few words she'd spoken told him something was troubling her.

"Ever hear of Extra Ordinary Designation Cards?"

"Nope," Castro answered.

"They give them to people with something wrong. What if they give me one . . . for my toes?"

The fact that his twin sister had twelve toes was a secret known only to the two of them and their parents. If she was worried, so was he. That's how it worked in those days.

"I'm going to tell Mom and Dad I want them removed."

But *she* had been removed, the express Castro reflected as he watched the boy slip under the covers.

Castro opened his eyes in the darkened, quiet warehouse bedroom. He was drenched in sweat and sick to his stomach. His heart was pounding hard—the cost of keeping her memory alive.

24

Pedro

Castro woke to a loud noise, like a wailing horn. How long had he taken to return to sleep after that jarring trip on the memory express? Though the symptoms had subsided, he still felt queasy and washed out.

Plodding down the corridor, Castro heard the sound grow louder. He felt a cool breeze. Looking up, he was startled to see a patch of thin gray light where a roof panel used to be.

Castro didn't meet anyone on his way to the lavatory, but after he'd dressed he encountered Clement and asked what had happened.

"Did you sleep through the storm? We had savage winds."

"How bad?"

"Awful," replied Clement, shaking his head. "I need your help. Most of the damage is more than we can handle. You must have seen the roof. The library façade and two house façades are down."

"When do you need me?"

"As soon as you're ready. Pedro's coming, too. He says if he can keep a big top anchored, he's up to anything." Wearing a worried frown, Clement added, "We'll see about that. Eat something first. This isn't just an hour's job."

In the kitchen, Castro met Sarah, who told him she had been awakened by the gale and couldn't get back to sleep.

"Be careful out there. Don't do anything stupid," she said to him.

"Pedro's coming with us."

"I don't trust him," she said. "I can't help it."

"I'd have expected Clement to be the skeptic. Remember how he grilled me?"

Castro met Pedro and the custodian by the warehouse door. Clement had put Last to work cleaning up debris that had fallen into the warehouse. "Hold on to your hats, boys," Clement hollered as he pushed open the door.

"Nothing like bad weather to expose every bad clamp, nail, and stake," Pedro remarked. "We should have brought fatty . . . for ballast."

The wind gripped Castro's jacket. He saw a façade leaning precariously. Leading the trio toward the park, Clement said, "Keep your eyes open for the roof panels. Hopefully, they haven't blown into the next county."

No sooner had the custodian said this than Castro saw two strips of metal, one about ten feet long and the other half that length, lodged against the façade of a house that fronted the park. The screenwriter was distressed to see that the grand oak had split in two, one half of the tree on the ground.

With the focus of a battlefield general, Clement ignored everything except for the roof panels. Out of the corner of his eye, Castro observed more devastation: the library façade was down and blocking half of Main Street.

"Put your gloves on. Castro, take the smaller piece. Pedro and I will tackle the big one."

The metal strips were vibrating like tuning forks in the gusty wind. Castro was relieved to see the pieces hadn't been badly deformed. As big as those sections were, and with the strong wind, carrying the panels wasn't easy. When a burst of wind wrenched the piece from Castro's hands, Pedro called out, "Don't turn the broadside into the wind, drag it on the ground . . . that's the style, brother!"

"We need to put these back on the roof and tack them

down," Clement yelled. "As long as that gap remains, the wind can dislodge more panels."

"Do you think it's safe up there?" Castro inquired.

"I'm sure it isn't, but I don't have a choice, do I?"

"I'll go up with you," Castro told the custodian.

"No thanks. I already have enough to worry about."

Fortunately, the wind was abating. Clement retrieved his riveting gun and the trio manhandled the panel pieces up the ladder without anyone taking a tumble or being gouged by sharp edges. Somehow, Clement pulled the two panels to the openings and tacked them down. After he'd descended, the weary and worried man informed Castro and Pedro that the panels were far from secure but might hold until the weather improved.

Castro said, "Has anyone inspected the garden?"

"Colleen went to take a look."

"How old is that dame anyway?" Pedro inquired.

"You try keeping up with her for a day," the custodian answered.

That afternoon, Clement and the residents tried to make up for the previous night's lost sleep or, in Castro's case, his rocky ride on the memory express. If he slept, it wasn't for long. Still, a quiet hour with closed eyes was welcome after that frantic morning.

In bed, Castro had been thinking about John Gray's love for the residents' garden, a place where the outcast had seemed to be at peace; recalling Gray's ornate birdhouses and sculpted birds, too.

The mirror in Gray's room was still covered. A glass half-filled with beer sat on the dressing table next to a vase of recently picked wildflowers. A few of the artist's birds were back on the table.

Castro wondered what seeing fear, revulsion, and horror in the eyes of everyone he encountered would be like. For all the misery Castro had experienced, he'd never been tempted to cover mirrors.

"Johnny had the eye, didn't he?"

How could a man as big as Max get so close without Castro hearing him?

"Johnny made a dozen studies of each bird before he touched a piece of wood." Last grinned. "I kept calling 'em sketches, and he kept calling 'em studies—what passes for humor around here.

"They wanted to clean the beer glass but I said leave it alone. When I first met John, I discovered that no matter how miserable you are, if you know someone more miserable, you feel a little better. But guess what? When we became friends, I learned that John's being happy didn't make me any less happy."

"They duped him," Castro said.

"Is that for my benefit? I already know that. I bet John did, too."

"Do you wish you were back in Texas?" Castro asked Last.

"Things I miss, things I don't. When I was a junior in high school, I was an all-state linebacker. In the bar, I said I wasn't stupid. One of my math teachers called me Maximilian the First because I was always at the top of my class."

Castro heard the change in Last's tone when he said, "In my senior year, everything went south. My stepfather pushed my mom around one time too many. I beat him up, so I had to leave town and live with my uncle. He ran the service department for the Phaetonic dealership in Waco. My uncle was as big as a house. By the time I learned my mom had 'fallen' down the stairs and died, I was too fat to make the bastard pay."

That this wasn't a chance meeting dawned on Castro. Last had sought him out. Urgency was in the air.

"Sarah said you're an orphan like me," Last observed. "Believe it or not, I'm glad you're trying to get Sarah out of here, but you didn't do the rest of us any favors by coming back."

The big man ambled over to Gray's wood carvings, stooped, and picked up an oriole as if it were a living thing. With his back to Castro, he said, "Take good care of Sarah. Don't break her heart. If you hurt her, I might have to slim down and come looking for you."

Last put the carving back on the table. "You'll write about us some day. When you do, sand off the rough edges . . . make me more than just a bitter slob."

Jumbo didn't give Castro a chance to reply. "Did you know Johnny had a wooden leg? It's true. I saw it, a real wooden leg from the knee down. Mahogany, not soft wood like these carvings. John told me he had to have his leg removed when he was a boy. Whenever his father took Johnny out, he told people they could see the leg for a dollar."

Castro recalled the young man struggling to keep up on their stormy dash to the warehouse. With John Gray, Castro had never been able to distinguish between truth and invention. "Do you believe his father used him to make money?"

"He might've. The leg I saw was perfectly shaped, Grigio and Son was carved into the wood. The knee and ankle joints were mechanical marvels."

Last glanced at the door and cleared his throat. "You spent the morning with Pedro. What do you think?"

"I wonder why Clement—"

"Takes up for that pompous little toad?" Last curtly interrupted.

This characterization was too much for Castro. "Pedro hasn't said or done anything suspicious."

The big man's face hardened. "His showing up out of the blue is suspicious enough for me."

"Have you ever known Clement to make a mistake with Red Cards?"

Last shook his head.

"Maybe we should give Clement and Pedro the benefit of the doubt."

"Who are you trying to convince?" Last retorted. "Me or yourself?"

The big man pulled out Mabel Drake's red chair and gingerly sat, exhaling an audible sigh. Prolonged standing had produced a sheen on his forehead and cheeks. The small chair was swallowed up in Jumbo's bulk, but the chair held, bringing grins to both men's faces.

"There's a science to this," Last observed. "Only a downward compressive force will do—never a shearing force. If mirrors were Johnny's enemy, gravity is mine."

Castro had learned more about Maximilian Last in the past twenty minutes than he had since arriving on the set, including the mechanic's math prowess. On a whim, he produced Muriel Martel's folded puzzle.

"Can you make anything of this?"

Jumbo unfolded the paper and stared at it like a man in a trance. After a minute, he looked up, and said, "It's a magic square."

Castro couldn't suppress a laugh.

"That's what it's called—magic square. I'll show you how it works. The magic number is fifteen. Every row, every column, every diagonal, sums to fifteen. That means the missing number is nine in the first row, and eight and six in the third row . . . It's true," he contended. "Put those numbers in the square and sum in any direction."

"What does it mean?" Castro pressed him.

Last shrugged. "The Chinese invented magic squares thousands of years ago, number puzzles the inventors believed had mystical properties." He handed the sheet back to Castro. "The person who prepared this square put some significance on the number fifteen. That's all I can tell you."

"You were the person who wrote S is greater than G on the wall."

Jumbo produced a thin smile.

"What does it mean, Max?"

"A mathematical representation of a universal human truth—scapegoating exceeds goodwill. The reason we're all trapped here."

Max lumbered to the dresser and lifted the beer glass. "Clement wants to see us in the library. I want to see him, too. Remember what I said about Sarah, pal."

The writer and the mechanic entered the library together. Pedro was in the chair next to Clement, kneeling on a cushion. The others were spread around the room.

Something about Castro's and Last's entrance put the others on alert.

"How's the garden?" Castro asked Colleen.

"Held up okay."

"Any damage—"

"I have something to say," Maximilian Last portentously announced. "I'm leaving."

"Oh, stuff and nonsense," Colleen said to him.

"We've been down this road before, Max," Clement said.

"It's different this time, Jeff. The SSB know we're here.

I'm getting out while the getting is good. You can drive me to Harrisville."

Castro heard an undertone of distress in Last's belligerence. The urgency Castro had felt in Gray's room now made sense.

Pedro said to Clement, "If he's loose in that little burg, you might as well attach a neon sign to this set announcing we're here."

"It's none of your business, shorty," Last griped, approaching the little man menacingly.

Clement stepped between the two.

"You'll have to drop him off in Bay City," Pedro said to Clement, as if Last weren't listening. "Detroit would be even better."

Jumbo's face was bright red. "Speaking of neon signs, explain why we're taking in a stranger when all hell's breaking loose?"

"Listen, Max, there's another hideaway," Clement said over his shoulder. "We aren't cooked yet, but after last night and repairing a roof in a windstorm, I'm not up to arguing with you. You have to trust me."

If there was another hideaway, Castro had seen no evidence of it on the engineering drawings.

"Max, please hold off for a few days," Colleen pleaded. "Just till things settle down?"

Last bestowed a warm look on the old woman. "And what makes you think things will settle down, Collie? After what Hume told us about the tunnel and with Johnny gone, we're finished, and you know it."

Clement shook his head and exited the room, followed by Pedro. A minute later, Last made for the kitchen in the opposite direction.

Fiona crept closer to Sarah, who took the the young woman's hand in hers. The mammalogist spoke up. "Let me re-cap today's lesson. The SSB know about the tunnel. Who knows what John has told them, or was made to tell them. And no matter what Jeff says, who knows if we can trust Pedro. Max may be a live wire, but at least he's a familiar one. Maybe he's smart to clear out."

"Jeff said there's another hideaway," Colleen countered.

"I heard him," Sarah responded. She turned to Castro. "Will the roof hold?" she asked.

"Unless we get another gale."

"C'mon Fi," Sarah said to the girl.

On her way out of the room, Sarah whispered in Castro's ear, "I'm glad you didn't get between Max and Pedro."

The screenwriter was alone in the library where Papa Drake had sought respite from life's storms.

What a stormy day today had been: the remnants of last night's memory express, a gale that had blown off part of the roof, Last's many revelations and imminent departure, and the Pedro enigma.

Castro sat at the table in the quiet room, retrieved the magic square from his pocket, and set it in front of him, adding the missing numbers Last had supplied.

4	9	2
3	5	7
8	1	6

As Last had said, every row, column, and diagonal summed to fifteen.

He had barely known Muriel Martel, and he barely knew Mary Fry, so why was he wasting time with that minor actress' disappearance?

Because he wasn't the same man he'd been six months before.

Max had claimed that the number fifteen had been significant to the puzzle maker. Why would fifteen be important to Muriel? Could fifteen refer to a date? If it did, how was Castro supposed to work out a solution? The fifteenth letter of the alphabet was O—what could that mean?

"What's that?" Fiona asked over Castro's shoulder.

"It's called a magic square," he answered without looking up.

"I love to count!" Fiona exclaimed.

He could always rely on Fiona to lift his spirits. "Sit next to me. You'll like this. When you add the numbers in any direction, you get the same answer."

She moved her finger over each row, column, and diagonal.

"Fifteen!" Fiona said eagerly. She moved her index finger in the air as if she were tracing letters on a book spine.

Suddenly, she gripped Castro's hand and pulled him from the chair. "More magic squares," she said.

He was now utterly confused. They moved as one to the actors' rooms where Fiona stopped in front of a door, moving her finger over the words on the nameplate.

KENNY MARKS, ACTOR

"Fifteen," she proudly proclaimed.

Five plus five plus five. Castro released the girl's hand and checked each of the other actor's doors. None of the other nameplate letters summed to fifteen.

He was still pondering this when Fiona pulled him along

to Gina's room and to Oscar's chest in the corner, tracing his name with her finger.

"Fifteen," Fiona solemnly said.

Kenny Marks' character: Oscar, the fifteenth letter of the alphabet.

25

Grave Matter

"Come with me," Sarah said to Castro.

A few wisps of auburn hair dangled from the mammalogist's scarf. She hadn't said much about her recovery, but what she'd said had been encouraging.

Castro followed Sarah to the northwest corner of the warehouse, where she turned west and crossed the strip of meadow that led into the woods somewhat north of where they'd entered the night of that harrowing trip to Detroit.

More leaves were on the ground and fewer on the trees with each passing day, though canopies remained mostly intact. Still visible in the failing light was a bright red carpet beneath the meadow's lone maple tree.

Mounds of leaves were piled against wood line tree trunks where the trillium bloomed in the spring.

Sarah seemed to know where she was going, removing a flashlight from her coat pocket and spraying the forest floor with light.

They hadn't gone far when Sarah stopped and held the light beam steady.

"Red baneberry," she said.

The small plant she'd illuminated displayed clusters of little red berries.

"Fiona collected wildflowers, then she and Gina would look them up in Gina's book. What do you think about Jeff's hideaway?" she asked him.

"I never heard a word about it when we were making

Stars, not even a rumor. I've seen the engineering drawings that show everything on the set including the tunnel."

"Why would Jeff make up something like that?"

"Unless he's trying to trick Max into staying," Castro speculated.

"Jeff's not the devious type."

"I didn't say that. But as Pedro pointed out, Max leaving the set would put everyone at risk."

"Pedro," she said meditatively. "What do we know about him? He hasn't told us much about himself, except that he was in the circus."

"Right. If there's another hideaway, Clement wasn't smart to reveal it with Pedro present. What's that?"

Both turned around. Sarah directed her flashlight at the sound.

A small creature emerged from the shadows.

"Ghost," Castro said. "Where have you been?"

"We're happy to see you, Ghost. We were worried about you," Sarah said soothingly.

The idomean didn't stir, nor did its big eyes.

"You know where we're going, Ghost," said Sarah. "Come with us."

The animal knew more than Castro about their destination. After that all night canoe trip, he supposed turnabout was fair play.

They'd been ascending a pine-needle-strewn incline. When they reached the crest, light from a full moon, supplemented by Sarah's flashlight, revealed an island of short grass.

"Gina's grave," she said, illuminating the flat stone.

Castro bent over and touched the stone. "She told me about her father—the man who rescued her."

Ghost had joined them. Sarah reached down and scratched the idomean's ear. "I know you loved Gina." To Castro she said, "When I moved here, Gina kept me from wallowing in self-pity."

The air was still. Moon shadows cast by taller trees streaked the hilltop.

"What does the word on Gina's wall mean?" asked Castro.

"Gina told me it means lamb, another name for the Logos."

Sarah's expression then turned somber. "After you'd left for L.A., I woke in the middle of the night, too anxious to sleep. I went to the kitchen for hot chocolate. Gina was in her wheelchair by the window. She had the hot chocolate on the stove before I realized she was doing the serving again."

"I wish I'd been with you," Castro interjected.

"I'm glad you weren't—or anyone else. That night, we needed each other. I'll never forget what she said to me. Gina knew I was a scientist and that I saw the world with a scientist's eye. She said that just as the law of gravity is necessary for stable galaxies, solar systems, and planets, so too the law of the gift—the more we give, the more we receive."

The idomean was on its haunches, as if it were on the alert.

"I don't buy it," Castro pushed back. "Gina was a gift to everyone here, so why was she made to suffer as she did? Why did she receive evil for her goodness?"

"I asked her that, too. Gina said the consequences of choices cascade from the person making the choice, as her mother's and adopted father's choices affected her . . . Do you hear something?" Sarah asked him, brushing needles off the gray stone.

Castro scanned the hilltop. He saw nothing apart from Sarah and Ghost.

"Gina said no one can nullify the law of the gift or the law of the choice, any more than they can nullify the law of gravity."

"Do you believe that?" he asked Sarah.

Instead of answering him, Sarah said, "You told me you didn't expect me to move in with you. Why should I go?"

He didn't know what to say to her. Rather, he didn't know whether to tell her the truth. All the other women he'd known, including Scarlet, had preferred ambiguity.

"I love you," he said.

"If I'm cured of cancer, I want to have children."

Her words startled him. What did children have to do with the two of them?

"I told you I love you."

"Are you asking me if that's enough? I want to know what you think about children."

He wasn't prepared for this. "My sister was killed. I was abandoned."

"You're afraid of having children because of what happened to you and your sister?"

Sarah didn't give him time to respond. "Would you rather live in a world of human animals created in SSB labs?"

"No!"

"Then who will create a different future if not people like us? Gina's law of the choice cuts both ways. Don't you see?"

Castro's lifelong conceit was that he saw more than ordinary people, the reason why Alfred Cooperwasser and Ron Starling had reached out to him. But hadn't she told him how that holiday with the Stewarts had changed her? Hadn't she been transfixed by that mother and her children in the Detroit park? Hadn't she told Castro the SSB would have to kill her before she let them harm Fiona? She had given him plenty of clues if only he had been paying attention.

Castro said, "What do you think creating a different future entails?"

"Gina's Red Card meant she couldn't attend school or receive therapy, so her adopted father spent hours with her every day posing questions about the natural and moral worlds, and then exploring those questions with her . . . Where's Ghost?" asked Sarah.

She searched the grassy hill with her beam. When she finally located the animal, Castro saw a white object at its feet. He hoped he was wrong, but when he walked over and pulled it from the sandy soil, it was as he feared, a leg or arm bone.

"You may be used to finding bones in the ground," he said to her. "Not me."

"Here's another one," Sarah said. "Unless I'm mistaken, this is a woman's pelvic bone. This isn't an erosive environment. The hill's not severely sloped. It's protected by tall trees. This was a shallow grave. The weather exposed these bones. I wonder who the poor girl was."

A sick feeling came over Castro. He was still processing what Sarah had said when he heard a rumbling growl.

Turning around, he saw the big bear loping toward them.

Sarah gripped his arm as Letta had once done.

How could he have forgotten about this monster or that night with Letta? How could he have let Sarah lead him into the forest at dusk?

Just as Castro went rigid with fear, Ghost appeared in the breach between them and the bear.

The bear stood still for a few moments before it slowly bypassed Ghost and came face to face with Sarah, whose eyes were closed.

This time, no window or exit separated the two.

The animal touched Sarah's forehead with its snout.

The jumble of emotions, sensations, and granular memories took Castro weeks to commit to words. The beast was huge and blind in one eye—the left. In the moonlight, its hair looked more blue than black.

Sarah extinguished the flashlight. Unbelievably, with her eyes still closed, she reached out and stroked that massive head.

Castro cringed. He couldn't make himself close his own eyes.

Her hand dropped to her side.

The undaunted idomean crept into the even smaller space between the bear and Sarah. Sitting on its haunches with its back to the woman, Ghost looked like a gray mouse beneath the huge bear's head.

When the bear trotted away—had it been one minute or ten?—the idomean rubbed against Castro's leg and began walking in the direction of the warehouse.

As vulnerable as he and Sarah had been, why hadn't that monster torn them limb from limb?

The pair followed Ghost, Castro's head on a swivel to make sure the bear wasn't pursuing them.

"Weren't you terrified?" Castro panted.

She sighed in return. "When you've been expecting cancer to eat you up a day at a time, a bear ending things in a few minutes doesn't seem so bad."

Ghost looked back at Castro and Sarah, as if urging them to hurry up.

What concatenation of purpose, foolishness, and weather, present and past, had caused Castro, Sarah, Ghost, the bear, and those exposed bones to be in that moonlit clearing at the same moment?

"Why were you asking so many questions about those bones?" Sarah asked him, reading his mind again.

He was pleased to see they weren't far from the set. "An actress with a small part in *Stars* disappeared during filming."

"You think those bones are hers?"

"If they aren't, it's an odd coincidence. A magic square suggests that conclusion."

"That sounds like something you'd say," she retorted.

"I hope I'm wrong. Why weren't those bones discovered when Gina was buried?"

Sarah took several steps before answering. "Let's say the woman has been in that shallow grave five or six years. The week Gina was buried we had torrential rains, so we were focused on the burial and staying as dry as we could. That heavy rain could have finished exposing the bones."

At the forest-meadow boundary, Sarah said, "I've decided to come with you. But it'll be hard on the others."

In the wake of the big bear, the mess of bones, and his complicated bond with Sarah, Castro wasn't surprised that sleep was elusive.

All the room lights had been extinguished. The warehouse was dark and silent, but Castro's mind was busy enough.

Of all things, his mind was fixed on what Sarah had related about Gina—his dead friend's descriptions of the law of the gift and the law of the choice, and how those principles had been unconsciously living in him.

Cooperwasser had become a surrogate father to him, Colleen a mother, Gina the sister Cynthia might have become had she lived; especially, his relationship with Sarah as compared to that tempestuous alliance with Scarlet—the gifts Cooperwasser, Colleen, Gina, and Sarah had been to him and, just as importantly, how those gifts had changed him.

When Castro finally fell asleep, he spent those few hours running through the forest, from what he knew not.

26

Invasion

Colleen burst into the dining room, shouting, "The set's crawling with Huns."

Castro knocked over his cup of coffee. Clement leapt up just in time to avoid a scalding.

"On my walk," she breathlessly said. "They're converging on the warehouse."

"Where's Pedro?" demanded Last. All of the residents were present in the parlor except for that dubious little man.

Clement said, "Don't go to your rooms. Follow me . . . now."

"Where?" asked Jumbo.

"The truck . . . now!"

Outside the live window, fog obscured everything. Last stood up and shook his head. "Not me, Jeff. I'll just slow you down. Get the others out of here."

Clement reached over and tugged on Fiona's ear.

Colleen said, "I'll lead them into the forest . . . if I can get that far. You have a truckload already." Not waiting for the custodian to reply, she marched down the corridor followed by big Last.

Clement said, "Come on," leading Fiona and Sarah toward the door. Castro caught up to Clement, and whispered, "Don't wait for me."

He turned down the hallway to the actors' rooms. When Sarah tried to grab his hand, he slapped hers away.

The dazed writer retrieved the rental car keys, put on a

jacket, and made for the rear door. As frantic as Castro was, his eyes were drawn like magnets to Maximilian Last's little equation on the wall: $S > G$.

As he had suspected, the rear door had been unlocked by Colleen because the SSB would have the tunnel exit guarded, if they weren't already inside the tunnel.

And whom would he meet outside this door? What other choice did he have? Perhaps he could use the fog as cover until he reached the woods.

Out the door he dashed, expecting to be challenged, but the fog was so thick he could see next to nothing—pure velvet for the residents who knew this site like the backs of their hands.

Permeating the still air was the scent of decaying leaves. Somewhere up above, a gyroplane was whirring. Castro saw a pair of lights, fuzzy yellow circles, a short distance away. A motor gunned loudly. Someone shouted, "Eight and six off."

He heard a holler, a cry of distress, and made for the sound. The timbre of the voice sounded familiar.

The phantasmagoric scene Castro saw when he reached the corner of the warehouse made him want to vomit. Screaming and flailing, Last was trying to fend off three large dogs. A fourth dog that had Ghost by the neck was shaking the idomean like a rag doll.

No sooner had Castro taken a step toward Last than the big man grabbed his chest with both hands, groaned, and sank to the ground. The fourth dog, having flung the lifeless Ghost away, joined the other three that were circling the motionless man.

Castro backed into the fog, crab-wise rather than a straight line. The lights he'd seen earlier had moved, or a new vehicle was parked to the west in the direction of the meadow.

The gyroplane sounded louder. Castro began to trot toward the forest. The vehicle lights, now red, were moving in front of him.

The thought of Sarah cornered like Last horrified him.

He reached the edge of the forest. Lying at his feet was a small bundle of gore. Castro recognized the shirt Pedro had worn the night he'd arrived on the set.

"The squirt got his just desserts," a voice at his side whispered. "Where's Max?"

His blank stare must have told Colleen enough. She just nodded. Lights converged on them.

"Are we going into the forest?" Castro asked.

Those killer dogs were making a racket.

"To be a good decoy, you have to get caught. *You* go, dear boy."

In this chaos, he recognized who Colleen really was, that rare person who preferred outright danger to uncertainty.

He heard a door shut, then another.

"Go!" she said.

Castro didn't move. Four figures came into view, all dressed in black and toting automatic weapons. One of them, a beetle-browed bulwark of a man a head taller than Castro, stirred the bag of bones on the ground with the barrel of his gun. "Who did this?"

Colleen squared her shoulders. "Maybe Nero or Caligula or whatever you call those hellhounds."

"The dogs didn't do this." The man spoke with a show of aggressiveness. "Where are the rest?"

The other three agents surrounded them. Colleen hesitated just long enough to create the impression that she was frightened, then she aimed her index finger at the woods. "They went in there."

"Who did?"

"The site manager and the girls. I was following them and couldn't keep up."

"Come with us. You, too," the bulwark said to Castro.

Castro cursed the man loudly. Instantly, he was struck on the forehead with something hard. The next thing he knew, his face was buried in a nest of pungent leaves. Dazed but still conscious, Castro heard one of the other men say, "The commander said hands off. That's the writer."

They dragged Castro to a caravan and deposited him in the back seat.

A minute later, he was herded into the library. Colleen was already in the room.

A square-jawed man at the table, two red officer bars on his black cap, said, "Where are the others?"

"Like I told fatso . . . in the forest," Colleen said fearlessly.

Someone behind them must have made a move in Colleen's direction because the officer raised a hand to ward him off.

"If they're in the forest, we'll find them," the officer brusquely responded.

A pair of young agents, cadets by their eager faces, boiled around the officer, as if waiting for an order. Castro felt cold disgust at these barbarians occupying his set, his library. Somehow, he had to bridle this feeling, for the others' sake if not his own.

Colleen said, "I'd be careful if I were you. Ask your boys about Pedro."

She was stalling. If Colleen could hold on, why couldn't Castro?

The officer glowered at him. "What are you doing here, Hume?"

He responded without delay. "Research."

"Cooperating with us is your ticket out of this mess. Is the old crone telling the truth?"

"I've never known her to lie."

The man's eyes moved from one captive to the other. "How do they expect to survive in the woods with no food or shelter?"

"Maybe they weren't thinking that far ahead," Castro responded, doing his utmost to play the part as Coop would have directed him to.

The man slammed his fist on the table. "If they were in the truck, where would Clement take them?"

"Miss Hardy said they went into the woods."

Castro happened to catch the eye of an agent across the room with his back to the shelves. This man, wearing an officer's cap with one bar, was surreptitiously shaking his head, as if conveying a silent warning to the prisoner. Was it possible that Brother Gerry had been less of an outlier than Castro imagined?

"Where would Clement take them?" the officer across from Castro roared.

"Harrisville, I suppose."

"That's the last place he'd take them." The officer stood and walked around the table, his face within inches of Castro's.

"I saw Pasternak get into the truck," one of the men at the door said.

Castro doubled down. "Where would Hardy have been going if she wasn't following the others?"

The officer looked at Colleen shrewdly. "Maybe she has a hero complex. Maybe you do, too."

A grin formed on the man's face. "Take Hume to Number One. The crone stays."

Castro's and Colleen's eyes met for a split second before two men grabbed his arms and hustled him out of the library.

Upon exiting the building, he immediately saw a parked Leviathan, larger than the others. The agents propelled Castro toward the vehicle, jerking him to a stop at the driver's door where the window descended, revealing Dana Philby in civilian clothes.

The fog was so heavy that sounds were muffled. Moisture coated the vehicle. Every few seconds, the Levia-pane wipers went down and up again.

The fog belied Castro's clear picture of what was going on here. Philby knew Castro and the rest were on the set, sending Pedro here meant she had Producer J in custody. What other reason could there be for the midget's appearance so soon before the raid and his absence that morning? This was intended to be an extermination mission, pure and simple. Fiona could be eliminated without drawing attention to the existential threat she posed to Philby. The SSB commander wanted her sister dead. And everyone else who might know of the family connection.

"Leave us alone," Philby said to the agents who had brought Castro to the caravan.

The pair immediately obeyed her.

Philby pointed at Castro's head. "Trip over a tree root?"

"If you think this is bad, you should see his face."

Philby ignored the remark. "Who was in the truck?"

Another Leviathan pulled up so quickly it ripped up turf. The driver hopped out and shot a glance at Castro.

"Go ahead," Philby ordered the agent.

"He got away, sir. Took a trail into the forest. Six and eight crashed and wrecked."

"Get a fix on Clement's phone," Philby ordered the man.

"He left it in the warehouse."

"What about the gyroplane?"

"Too much fog. He's heading back to Alpena."

"Was the imbecile with Clement?"

It was all Castro could do to restrain himself.

"We think so."

Philby reached out her window and put a finger in the agent's face. "Clement'll hide in the woods until we leave. Bring in the backhoes and dozers. Start digging. I want to find that hideaway of his."

"Yes, sir."

"Now! Move it!"

The man ran off like a scared rabbit.

Two gunshots split the air.

"Your doing," Philby said to Castro with a shrug. He hated himself for that split second when he had hoped Colleen had taken the hit. But even if she had been the victim this time, how long before the others would have their turn?

A late-season bee buzzed at his ear, so close he could feel it crawling on the lobe. He'd always been afraid of bee stings.

Philby looked hard at Castro, "By the way, you're not the only one with a trophy on your shelf. I have a wooden leg on mine."

The longer Castro delayed Philby and her team, the better for Clement, Sarah, and Fi. "Where's Colleen Hardy?" he asked.

"You're a man of words, Hume, so you should understand this." She calmly produced an automatic pistol and pointed the weapon at Castro's head. "This speaks exactly six words. But I doubt more than one will be necessary."

Castro shuddered with fear. It was now or never if the screenwriter was going to flip the script. He had to look and sound the part, no matter how scared and angry he was. What had Benson said to him when they had argued about Stephen Drake's response to the Oscar killed-in-action telegram? "You can't sell it to the audience if you can't sell it to yourself."

"That first day, you left blood on a warehouse door handle," Castro said as calmly as he could. Her plastic face was immobile, but her mind was racing. He could see it in her eyes.

Don't let her off the mat, he told himself. "The blood sample proves you have a damaged—a Red Card—sister."

The commander lowered the pistol. "No one will believe you," Philby hissed.

"Can you take that chance?" He knew she couldn't.

This woman could have asked how he knew it was her blood? Why had he analyzed the blood in the first place? Why didn't she remember the wound? But asking such questions would bring Dana Philby into closer proximity to Phiona Philby, something the commander must avoid at all costs.

"Don't think if I'm eliminated this information won't be communicated. The same goes for eliminating those three in the truck. Call off your manhunt or else."

Philby gave him a withering look. "Get out of here!"

For a moment, Philby's mask slipped, and Castro saw in her face the same rage and humiliation felt by the sixteen-year-old consigned once again to his aunt's basement.

He did what he always did when he was on his heels. He defaulted to contrived levity. Castro took two steps, looked over his shoulder, and said, "What are you going to do about my idomean?"

27

Harbinger

The morning after Castro's return to California, Ron Starling showed up on his doorstep in a wheelchair, assisted, not by SSB Mark, but by a young woman with green hair.

If the visitor was put off by Castro's living quarters, he hid it well. Castro had thrown on the brocade dressing gown that Claude Benson, who had seen his own share of ups and downs, had given him for his birthday. Otherwise, Castro looked as if he had just rolled out of bed, which he had.

"I can't thank you enough for Sarah," Castro said.

Starling waved him off, then stretched out his hand.

Castro handed over the script for the stage play.

"That's what I call a title," Starling said.

Castro's hero looked as fragile as a daddy longlegs. "Would you like some coffee?" Castro asked. "Black? I haven't had time to buy groceries."

"I'd like a cigarette and a glass of bourbon—I'm returning to my foxhole. This script had to pass from your hand to mine. You understand what I mean."

With great effort, Starling lifted himself from the chair and took several steps. "Come closer," he said in a wheezy whisper. With a sardonic grin, the old man went on. "As you're wearing my mantle and as we're removed from Mark and the house, I'll tell you a deep, dark secret."

The daddy longlegs looked over his shoulder at the green-haired girl and lost his balance. Castro righted Starling by gripping the man's shoulder. "I'll help you back to your chair."

"No, you won't!" Starling hissed. "Lisa's my granddaughter. She passes messages to and from a confederation of politicals, artists, scientists, railroad conductors . . . and a few other mischief makers, some more dependable than others. Handwritten messages—mundane subjects."

He took a series of fortifying breaths. "A single dot on an *i* or a period at the end of a sentence contains the real message, but you need special glasses invented by one of our scientists to read the—." He hacked several times and whispered, "Read the secret messages."

Castro hadn't released Starling's shoulder, nor had the prickly old man shaken him off.

Lisa walked over to a window and looked up and down the street.

"Who's directing this confederation?" Castro asked.

"Herding those cats? I assembled them. Took years. Whoever's best suited takes the lead. Harder to behead a hydra than a snake. From now on, if I have anything for you, I'll send Lisa with the message . . . Take a long look at Lisa. Go ahead. She's expecting it. Imagine you're writing her character."

When the woman saw Castro looking at her, she ceased her head-pivoting surveillance and faced him head-on.

Starling slowly backed into his wheelchair and turned it toward the door. Without a word, Lisa pushed him over the threshold and into the parking lot.

28

The Director

October

Castro had received a call from Alfred Cooperwasser requesting that they meet in a park near the director's Beverly Hills home. The screenwriter was halfway around the walking trail when he spotted Cooperwasser seated on a bench.

The filmmaker stood and adjusted his copper-colored bowtie, a smaller neckpiece than the one he'd worn at the Saint-Tropez.

"I'll join you, Castro."

Cooperwasser had never impressed Castro as a walker. Worrying a button on his jacket, the man said, "Listen, I have a closetful of gouache posters we made for *Stars*. As I recall, you composed all those straplines. Say the word, and I'll send one over."

"I'd like one," Castro said

"Have you heard Francesco's gone missing?"

Castro gave the director an unbelieving look. "They wouldn't dare –"

"You'll not see anything about it in the news. He spoke out of turn and was removed. You were in Michigan at the time."

"What did he do?"

"Do?" Cooperwasser mused. "He dared to compose and distribute a tract opposing the SSB."

"Where is he, Coop?"

"Somewhere, I imagine, where even the illustrious Cap—that illustrious name—has no effect. I relate this troubling news because I've heard you're composing a stage play," said the director with deepening gravity.

Was this the reason Cooperwasser had invited him here? "That's right. A version of the script I'm working on . . . for community theater."

Cooperwasser wagged a finger. "Be careful. You have a co-writer, I understand. Is that old buzzard still smoking like a chimney?"

Had Cooperwasser said buzzard or wizard? Castro was reluctant to ask. "He's unwell. That may be his only remaining pleasure."

"Not if he still has some of the Lafitte in his wine cellar," returned the director. "And make no mistake, my boy, he still has a few arrows in his quiver. One of them might answer to a name that rhymes with *doom*."

Dr. Weems is another one of those arrows, Castro ruminated. "Have you heard of Red Cards?" he asked.

Cooperwasser exhibited a frown. "Enough to know I don't want one."

"White Cards?"

The director shook his head.

They strolled in an uncomfortable silence until the older man said, "The Bureau flew me to the set last week."

Castro didn't have to ask which set. Only a few walkers were about, none close enough to hear their conversation, or so he hoped.

"The Bureau was interested in concealed structures on or near the set. They asked questions about you. I believe I was sufficiently obscure. The set's been demolished, the warehouse, too. Excavation craters everywhere. Part of the forest bulldozed. I'm used to seeing sets torn down, so it didn't bother me. The place reminded me of the first month before we built anything, when the contractors plowed down trees and leveled the ground. In twenty years, the trees will be back. That's the way it ought to be, Castro. The photoplay is the thing, not the set."

Cooperwasser's contractors hadn't plowed down the fruit trees. The Red Cards' garden and trees remained in Castro's mental album of the set. "Did they bring any large animals out of the forest?" he asked.

Cooperwasser's brow furrowed. He stopped walking and looked around. "None that I saw. Armed agents were going in and out of the woods, some of them with big dogs and overnight packs."

"If a little mayhem is good, more is better."

The director responded with his rare little laugh—"Hoh hoh . . . That's a line worth hanging onto, my boy."

Did the SSB know about the bear? Castro found himself hoping the animal had escaped, for the service it had likely rendered in the matter of Pedro, if nothing else.

"They escorted me around the site, went over the blueprints, asked questions about contractors and architects. All nonsense. Making a mess for the sake of . . . mayhem. Why do you think we're trudging around this godawful park when I have comfortable chairs in my studio office? Because I don't trust my lovely niece, Dana, or her cohorts. Walt Whitman was right. *They are reptiles marking their paths with slime wherever they go.*"

Cooperwasser went on. "Before an agent realized I wasn't one of them, he mentioned they'd arrested the site manager's Bureau collaborator some months before."

As Castro had suspected, the SSB had delayed their invasion until they'd identified the mole within the Bureau.

Then they deployed their own mole, Pedro, to make sure their dragnet was complete. And it would have been except for the soupy fog and the courage of Clement and the Red Cards.

"Does your niece have a younger sister?" Castro asked as nonchalantly as he could.

Cooperwasser wasn't fooled. For a minute, Castro didn't think he'd get an answer. "I'm not accustomed to being peppered with personal questions, Mr. Hume."

"I'm sorry, Coop. Someone in Michigan accused me of presuming to be a shepherd boy out to slay the armored giant."

"Perhaps that was a compliment," was the director's surprising reply.

"That's not how I took it."

"That's because you haven't studied the script. Prior to battling the giant, didn't the young man inform the king that to protect his flock he'd killed lions and bears? How do you think that young man brought down such fearsome beasts? The answer is that boy was far deadlier with his sling than the giant with his armor and sword.

"You smile, but the giant would have to run down his nimbler adversary. If the shepherd boy misfired, he needed only to reload. So, who was the underdog, eh?"

The director let a young hand-in-hand couple pass. "Dana is actually a second or third cousin. I call her my niece because it flatters her and doesn't cost me anything. As I recall, she grew up in Massachusetts. She has never mentioned siblings. I took her to be an only child. The less you—and I for that matter—have to do with my niece, the better. Weren't you listening when I told you what they did to the set?"

He put a hand on Castro's shoulder. "We had a nice run with *Stars*. We made a revered book into a revered photoplay. I'd like to see you back on your feet again, pursuing your art. Aren't the pain and disappointment of life somewhat assuaged by art?"

His companion's question stirred something in Castro. "Mightn't there be something higher than art?"

The director hummed softly. "Have you seen anything higher in this world?" The filmmaker didn't wait for him to answer. "If you have, I'd be glad to hear it. Until then, art will have to do. Speaking of art, I discovered a painting they removed from the warehouse. I told those Bureau people it belonged to me. An unsettling piece to say the least, but perhaps you were acquainted with the artist. Perhaps it has sentimental value."

"I would like to have it," Castro said, guessing the art was connected to John's *Dorian Gray* project.

"I'll have the painting delivered," Cooperwasser said. "If the picture troubles you, dispose of it. I certainly would."

"Marks left the set in a hurry. Do you know why?"

"Good God!" the director thundered. "I'm beginning to regret this tête-à-tête. If you pursue such things, you will have more to worry about than your career. I could say Mr. Marks left in a confusing rush and inconvenienced me. He told me he was sick . . . had to see a specialist here."

"Did you believe him?"

"No. Marks wanted to be rid of our backwoods accommodations."

The other actors, too, had been chomping at the bit to flee the set, but a sense of what Cooperwasser's photoplay would do for their careers had kept them engaged.

"However," the director went on, "I was later informed by a reliable source that Marks had indeed taken ill, infected by a bacterium conveyed by a tick found in Michigan forests. He was ill for several months."

Everything fit, including Dr. Locard's principle. Marks had brought the victim, Muriel Martel, to the crime scene and had taken away an infected tick.

"Kenny Marks was the last person to have frolicked in that forest," Castro countered. "He wouldn't have gone into those woods for love or money."

Cooperwasser gave Castro a sidelong glance. "I concur. Never for love or money. You see, I learned all this months later, long after I'd left the set. You could say I possessed a few frames of film, a few lines of script from a scene that was suggestive of a dark theme. Tell me what's going on."

Castro resolutely shook his head. "If I told you, you'd be living in a dime store apartment like me, with big black trucks camped outside your door."

"My dear Castro, I'm delighted to see you still have a way with words. Do you know why I chose you for *Stars Too Bright*?"

Apparently, Castro hadn't aggravated the maestro enough because before giving his words due consideration, he said, "I've been told so you could write the screenplay yourself."

"You've been told that by fools," Cooperwasser snapped. "I contributed less to the *Stars Too Bright* screenplay than any of my other projects."

While filming *Stars,* the old master would occasionally commission a lift-all, directing a scene from thirty or forty feet in the air, sitting like a buddha in his camp chair. Once, he'd invited Castro to stand next to him as they shot a scene. No one else had ever enjoyed that privilege, not even the imageographer, Berkowitz.

Cooperwasser jarringly broke into Castro's recollection: "If battle you must, use your sling."

29

A Girl's Life

Nineteen years earlier

Dana imagined herself at her graduation three years hence receiving the First Athena golden helm.

The sixteen-year old was a block into her walk home from Athena Women's Academy, an all-urban route of just over a mile. As Dana had no other means of transportation, she had to be prepared for every kind of weather—today's benign enough for a light jacket beneath her waterproof backpack.

The Athena was a private school well beyond the means of Dana's working-class parents. Half her parents' small bedroom was taken up by her mother's needlework, commissions that served Dana's wealthy classmates. Often, the girl would wake in the middle of the night to find her mother under a dim lamp, needle and thread in hand. Even as Dana recognized how important her mother's late-night work was to their family, she had vowed never to be like her.

All of her classmates were debutantes, while the debut of Dana's more mature physique had been hailed by the leers and catcalls of the denizens of her family's tenement.

Only her mother's appeal to a wealthy cousin had made an Athena education possible for Dana. In fact, "Aunt Cooperwasser" had done more than that because money hadn't been the only obstacle for a girl outside the Athena's privileged social circle.

When Dana had learned she would be attending the Athena, she could scarcely believe her good fortune, convinced the humiliation of living in the tiny Philby apartment would soon be remedied. Fortunately, her usual attire wouldn't draw attention at school because all the girls wore uniform blue slacks and gold blouses.

The shops and townhomes along the first third of Dana's route home were reserved for Boston's brahmins. In the midst of the boutiques was a corpus augere. More than a few of Dana's classmates had bragged about corpus augere to correct flaws or to enhance physical features.

"Will you talk to Aunt Cooperwasser?" Dana had asked her mother after hearing that Lois' augere had earned her a place in the Theater Nouveau.

"What would I say to her?"

"Make something up."

"You're not bad looking, Dana," her mother had said.

Occasionally, when the weather was agreeable, Dana would window shop, imagining a life in which entering these high-end stores would come naturally to her. No such fantasies today. Dana had too much on her mind. She would need all her strength and wits for the mission she would undertake when she got home. And how necessary that mission was.

"Your sister's a trisomy 21 . . . a Red Card."

"Who told you that?"

"We saw her with you and your parents."

"She isn't my sister."

"Who is that imbecile, then?"

"We're keeping her for a friend."

"Your father was holding her hand."

"That's just his way. We don't care about her."

As the hectoring trio marched away, one of the girls said, "Nothing but swamp life." The other girls erupted in laughter.

From that moment on, Dana had decided that Phiona must go. She had done her research. She knew trisomy 21 wasn't inherited. Yet, the fact remained she had a visibly defective sister—"Nothing but swamp life." How could that fact not affect Dana now and in the future?

As if Dana's parents weren't enough of a disgrace, she had to suffer this other humiliation. Bad enough that she had been excluded from the academy's social circle on account of her parents; Phiona had multiplied the opprobrium.

Dana entered the transitional zone between the wealthy district and the beehive apartments where her parents lived. Here, trendy boutiques stood side-by-side with cut-rate shops.

She came to the busiest corner on the route. More than once, a vehicle had ignored the brightly painted GIVE-WAY and had almost struck her. And sure enough, an ultramarine Phaetonic zoomed through the intersection. She wondered if the driver heard the stone—kept in her pocket for such outrageous behavior—rattle off the rear bumper.

Plan well ahead was Dana's motto.

The GIVE-WAY reminded Dana of her first meeting with the headmistress, when the girl had to summon all her self-discipline in the face of that woman's truculence.

"I've been told you're something of a firefly."

"No, Ma'am."

"I've been told Alfred Cooperwasser is your patron."

Without hesitation: "Yes, Ma'am."

"Do you think that matters at this academy?"

Without hesitation: "No, Ma'am."

Of course, her connection to Alfred Cooperwasser mattered. Dana could see it in the woman's eyes. How much the connection mattered remained to be seen.

"Your leash is this long." The space between the gorgon's thumb and index finger measured less than an inch.

"Yes, Ma'am."

"Don't ever forget this, not for one minute."

"No, Ma'am, I won't forget," said the girl docilely with an inner resolution someday—a year from now or ten—to bring this woman to her knees.

After that encounter, Dana had been convinced the gorgon had stored up vitriol she couldn't expend on the privileged girls until she could unload it on someone like Dana.

Dana had done her best to counter the disdain her state in life provoked in her classmates and teachers by letting it be known that she was related to Alfred Cooperwasser, the up-and-coming director. She failed to mention that the relationship was distant and by marriage and that she had never met him. Though Dana had remained an outsider, the Alfred Cooperwasser connection meant her classmates dared not kick her too hard. After all, more than a few of the girls would gladly have given up their maidenhood to be cast in a Cooperwasser photoplay.

Unlike Dana's other classmates, Corinna had been quick to befriend her. Corinna didn't seem to care what the others thought of her—"You don't have to be like them."

Easy for Corinna to say. Her mother was an academy matriarch, and her father was the most prestigious furrier in Massachusetts.

In the end, Dana had concluded that Corinna would be an impediment rather than an asset. Dana now avoided the girl.

Impediments were always on her mind these days, Phiona at the top of the list.

Her two-year-old sister had an Extraordinary Designation Card, and unless Dana took charge, her parents would muddle along with the child. What had been the point of worming her way into the academy if Dana was to be shunned because of Phiona?

Dana remembered that last conversation with Corinna:

"She's your sister, isn't she?"

"Of course not!"

"You needn't be ashamed of her."

"We're keeping her for a bit, that's all. She'll be gone soon. Don't spread lies about me."

After Phiona was born, Dana was happy to have a sister. Even after Dana realized that Phiona was damaged, she was drawn to the infant. But Dana's quest to attend the Athena and her ardent desire to be respected by her classmates drove all affection for Phiona out of her.

The girl was a threat.

Dana crossed into what the Athenas called the dirty-hands district, where the residents did manual labor ten or twelve or more hours a day to earn their meager livings.

The zone where Dana's family lived.

The zone she was determined to escape at all costs.

"No! No! . . . No!" the red-faced woman screamed that evening.

The man at her side said, "Tell us exactly what happened."

How many times had Dana practiced for this moment? Whenever her resolve weakened, she had recalled the miserable hovel where she lived.

"I was holding her hand like you told me," she said. "A car stopped at the curb next to us. Two men jumped out.

One of them grabbed me and threw me down."

Dana showed her parents her bruised arm and bloody knee. "The other man took Phiona and put her in the car. Then they hurried off. There was nothing I could do."

"Of course not, dear," the woman sobbed.

"What kind of car?" the man demanded.

"Phaetonic. Uptown, I guess."

"What color?"

"Black." Dana knew he didn't believe her but couldn't prove otherwise. She had planned too well.

The weeping woman had sunk to her knees.

"License plate?" asked the man.

Dana shook her head.

"Not a single number?" He spat a curse and turned away.

"Call the police," the woman pleaded.

"Sure," the man muttered.

He pivoted back to the girl. "The police won't find her, will they, Dana?" asked the man in a low voice only he and his daughter could hear.

PART III

David

30

Accolades

The previous night, for the umpteenth time, Castro had to tell someone he couldn't share a drink with them because he was an alcoholic. And for the umpteenth time, that admission wasn't as easy as he had represented it to be.

Castro sat on a card-table chair in a dim, claustrophobic room. His cardboard Red Card lay on the table. How long would it be until he received a real one, as Gina's rebellious father had?

Perhaps Dana Philby had already learned his blood sample linking the two Philby women was a colossal bluff.

He had scrounged up the props for the play at second-hand shops, and the backcloths had been prepared by a friend of Alfred Cooperwasser's at a steep discount. The hungry actors who had also been recruited by Cooperwasser had agreed to work for a percentage of the box office. If Ba Jin was right, they'd be even hungrier after this production.

"My only requirement is that you keep my name off the playbill," Cooperwasser had insisted.

Though Castro's characters were now encased in the writer's imaginative amber, the flesh and blood people who had inspired those characters continued to surprise him. The painting Cooperwasser had rescued from the set was a riot of blacks, vomitous greens, grays, and blood reds—a maelstrom, a field of carnage—jarring to the eye. How shocked he'd been to see the initials in the lower right of the painting: GM—Gina Miller.

Was this picture how his friend had seen the world with her inner eye? How could the Gina he had known produce such a horror?

As much as the painting had troubled him, Castro had been unable to destroy it, so he had placed it on the apartment floor with the image facing the wall.

Snatching the playbill from the card table, Castro walked out the door and down the aisle toward the stage. Excited and apprehensive, he was hoping for a full house that evening.

He was sure the SSB would be represented, taking names and recording every word.

Castro couldn't stop thinking about Clement, Fiona, and Sarah—especially Sarah. Where were they? Were they alive? As always, his stomach lurched at such questions.

He looked out at the theater, then at the playbill he was holding: *Seeing Red*, by C. Hume and R. Starling.

Starling had insisted that Castro get top billing. Castro ardently hoped the old man would make it to the premiere as he had promised. When Starling returned the script via that green-haired woman, he had handwritten, *Way to go, kid!* on the title page. *That's what I call writing to a deadline!*

At seven, the theater was full and the lights had been dimmed. From the wings, Castro watched Starling's attendant, Mark, wheel the old man to the front, prompting a standing ovation Starling tried to ignore and finally acknowledged with a half-raised hand.

Recalling what Starling had revealed about Mark, Castro was surprised Lisa hadn't accompanied her grandfather to the theater.

Five minutes before intermission, Mark wheeled Starling out of the theater. From the wings, it seemed to Castro that the old man was shaking his head all the way to the back of the theater. All eyes had shifted from the performance on stage to the abrupt departure of the co-author of the play.

Castro made a move to exit the wings, intending to race up the aisle and confront the man in the wheelchair. At that moment, someone called out in a commanding voice, "Kill the lights!"

31

The Philistine

November

A month had elapsed since opening night at that Los Angeles theater.

The mechanic two blocks from the apartment had done what he could with the five hundred dollars Castro could afford to spend. When the writer had asked if the car would make it to New York—he was wary of identifying Michigan as his destination—the mechanic had given him slightly better odds of arriving than not.

Castro had departed L.A. in the middle of the night without telling a single soul he was leaving. Even so, he had expected the SSB to be following or tracking him.

Something in the front of the vehicle had commenced rattling in western Nebraska, but that was the least of his worries as there was nothing to be done about it.

Tonight, Castro was lodging in a ten-by-ten hotel room in middle Iowa. The next day he would be in Michigan.

He had tried to talk to Ron Starling—without success. A visit to the man's house hadn't elicited any response, either. Had the person in the wheelchair on opening night been Starling or an impostor recruited by the SSB?

Two days before Castro left California, a green-haired woman had come to his apartment with a message from Starling—a verbal message, as the impresario had dared not commit anything to writing, she said.

"Don't try to contact me," the woman claimed Starling

had said. "It's too dangerous. I'll contact you when the time is right. In the meantime, you'll be safer if you remove my name from the stage play."

Castro remembered Starling's words when he had visited his apartment with his green-haired granddaughter. *Take a long look at Lisa. Go ahead. She's expecting it. Imagine you're writing her character.*

He had looked keenly at the messenger before him and realized that she wasn't Lisa.

Out of his satchel, Castro removed a hand-addressed envelope, postmarked Louisville, Kentucky, containing no return address. Inside was a folded newspaper ad, not identifying the publication or the date.

A FOLLY IN THE WOODS:

EXQUISITE HUNTING AND FISHING CAMP FOR SALE

Built on five majestically wooded, exquisitely canopied acres, feet of living space and accommodations for up to 10. Built to last with steel and concrete construction, and built to impress with finished log and fieldstone exterior. The structure and slate roof are sound, and the site is equipped with a productive water well and septic/tile field. This refuge is perfect for the serious hunter, fisherman, or naturalist. Accessible by 4-wheel drive vehicles via a one-lane-trail.

The following morning, the writer slept later than he had intended. On the way out of town, he grabbed a coffee and a pastry.

The long, lonely trip and constant worry had caught up with Castro. He had felt off-color that morning but had forced himself to push on, arriving in Tawas City by dinnertime. After a hearty meal—when would he enjoy another?—he located the motor hotel on the edge of town and checked in, requesting a room facing the woods.

Having locked the door, Castro removed some things from his travel bag, put the car keys and his phone in an envelope, and taped them to the bottom of the table.

He had several hours to wait. His nerves were raw from not knowing what awaited him that night.

The soft tapping at the door sent his pulse racing.

"It's me . . . Mary," the voice on the other side said.

Castro let in Mary Fry and locked the door behind her. He had contacted the *Stars Too Bright* production assistant before leaving L.A., telling her nothing except for where and when to meet him.

"I can't stay long," she said.

Nor should she, he was tempted to say.

"Have you learned something about Muriel?" she asked eagerly.

"Maybe. Are you sure you want to hear it?"

Mary Fry nodded resolutely.

Castro tried to calm himself, but the effort was useless. He had too much on his mind. "Kenny Marks had one of the principal actors' rooms inside the warehouse. I remember seeing him bring a woman there, maybe Muriel. Not long after that night, Marks left the set in a hurry."

Mary's face fell. "What aren't you telling me?"

"I discovered a shallow grave in the woods. Nothing but a mess of bones."

"A woman?"

He nodded.

Mary teared up. "I'll never forget Muriel. I have so many good memories of us growing up together."

"A friend told me memories can keep my dead sister alive," Castro said in an attempt to encourage her.

Mary looked away for a moment, then she locked eyes with Castro. "Alive in your memory. The Logos promises a life that makes anything we experience here pale in comparison." Mary Fry reached over and took his hand in both of hers. "Your sister may be enjoying that life."

Her touch and words produced a jolt that brought tears to his eyes. She released him and stepped back, as if she'd taken an undue liberty.

Anticipating Mary's visit on the road to Michigan, Castro had had plenty of time to ponder the Muriel mystery: the bones he and Sarah had found, what Cooperwasser had said about Marks' sudden departure from the set. Near the Indiana-Michigan border, something else came to him, the memory he had been trying to retrieve when he had met Mary Fry in the diner—the snippet of conversation Castro had heard between Claude Benson and Brian Bergin the night with Letta and the wolves:

"Kenny insists she's a receptive dish."

"The local kid, right?"

Who else could that *local kid* have been, if not Muriel Martel? Had Kenny Marks impregnated and then killed Muriel when she threatened the star with trouble? Or maybe Marks had decided on a preemptive strike.

When Castro shared the memory with Mary, her jaw dropped. "So, Marks is worse than a seducer," she said. "He's a murderer, too."

She reached into her pocket and handed him a medallion with the head of a man crowned with something like a wreath on one side and a flame on the other. "Take this. Keep it with you."

Her hand was on the doorknob when Castro called out, "Mary!"

She turned back to him.

"My friend wrote the word 'lamb' on her wall, but to me

Gina was a lion." In fact, Castro was asking this woman a question that had been troubling him.

Mary Fry said, "Perhaps one can be both, according to need."

The day before he left California, Castro had carried Gina Miller's painting to the apartments' rubbish bin. One last look, he had told himself, in memory of his friend. Only then, in the daylight—the morning light—had he recognized the spiderweb-thin golden thread woven through the entire painting.

Mary opened the door, turned back, and asked, "Did you receive Muriel's puzzle?"

Castro nodded.

"Something to distract me, I suppose. That was Muriel," she said on the way out.

At almost midnight, Castro Hume, wearing black from head to toe, opened the motel window and climbed out. He ran as fast as he could toward the wood line and was soon amidst the trees. He had a small pack on his back and a compass in his hand.

He faced a three-mile hike. That was if he took a straight line. Who was this Castro Hume, this stranger? he asked himself.

Marching deeper into the woods, Castro was still thinking about Mary Fry, Muriel Martel, and Kenny Marks. Had Marks gotten away with murder? He made a determined effort at mental recall—the brightly lit, festive tent where Cooperwasser had hosted all the actors the evening Castro arrived on the set. One big happy family. Now, Letta drowned, Brian Bergin rumored to be deadly ill, Muriel reduced to bones, the murderer Kenny Marks in great demand. Don't forget Hume, he told himself, barely a step ahead of the SSB.

The river, wider than he had expected, glimmered in the moonlight.

What looked like silver spears piercing the water were oars propelling a boat coming toward him. A figure stood up in the boat, bracing itself with an oar.

"Don't just stand there, get in," Evan Masters said with a grin.

Castro stationed himself in the front of the boat.

"Don't think we're safe in the dark or in these woods," Masters whispered, stowing the oars and engaging the motor.

The boat moved upriver so slowly it barely made a wake. "How'd you escape the set?" Masters asked.

Without supplying all the details, Castro related how he'd bluffed Philby into letting him go.

Masters gave him a one-word response: "Courage."

"Or desperation," Castro countered.

"They're often the same," the pilot fired back. "Sleep if you want to. I have plenty of coffee to keep me going."

Castro said, "When I get to—"

"I don't want to know any more about it," Masters interrupted him.

"When I get to where I'm going, I'll tell them how much help you've been."

Castro had never seen this man when he wasn't on the water. "You know my story," Masters reminded him. "Tell me why someone who doesn't have a Red Card is taking such a risk."

Wasn't that the question Castro had asked himself before he left California?

"Because they need me and because the love of my life is there."

"I figured as much, but I wanted to hear you say it."

Pointing up ahead, Masters said, "That's our stream, I think. Let me see the map. You keep her in the channel."

A minute later, Masters said, "That's it . . . right where it's supposed to be."

Navigating the stream, they had to go even more slowly. When reed thickets crowded the channel, Masters deftly weaved around denser beds.

By this time, a cool, clear autumn morning was breaking.

"Not much farther, unless we want to ground or bind her," the pilot announced.

"Put me off on the right bank," Castro advised him.

Masters found a pool clear of weeds and eased in. "Here," he said, handing Castro a waterproof envelope. "Compass points and route landmarks. Jeff said you'll have to hurry to make it by nightfall."

His feet moist from the first few steps, Castro waited until Masters had turned the boat around and started back. He was now utterly reliant on his compass and instructions.

He saw few animals, probably because of the racket he was making.

He hiked through stretches where the land was hilly and other stretches where thick brush required left-right traversing. He had to cross two shallow creeks, taking off his shoes and rolling up his pant legs—a third he was able to ford on a fallen tree trunk.

Not far from this third stream, Castro exited the woods into a wide meadow bathed in sunlight and spotted with end-of-year goldenrod and purple blazing star. The pale grass was as fine as human hair, and when the wind stirred, the grass moved like waves on a lake. He stopped, closed his eyes, and took a deep breath.

Without warning, he felt pressure between his collarbones. An all-too-familiar voice said, "You're going to take me to them."

Castro's heart thumped like a kettledrum. He turned to see Dana Philby, pistol in hand, wearing camouflage gear. Her face was expressionless.

"I know Clement's rat hole is nearby. I'll find it with or without you. Move or I'll kill you right here. Don't think I won't."

He knew Philby was no less deadly here than in that Leviathan on the set when she was commanding dozens of storm troopers.

This time, Castro had no script to flip, and by the look on the commander's face, nothing he could say would deter her. She and her pistol would have the last word.

"I'm not moving."

"You don't fool me, Hume. You're a coward who threw what little talent he had out the window."

"Ron Starling and Alfred Cooperwasser don't think so."

"That wasn't my blood, but you know that." She raised the pistol and pulled the trigger.

Castro shuddered. His knees buckled. Nothing happened.

If he hadn't seen the stunned expression on Philby's face, he would have believed she was toying with him.

Dana Philby ejected the bad clip and was slamming home a new one.

He heard his mother's voice: "Your Uncle Castro always said, 'If a fight can't be avoided, you have to throw the first punch.'"

Castro slammed his fist into Philby's face with his full weight behind it, producing a loud crack.

The SSB commander collapsed like a rag doll, blood streaming from her nose and eyes.

He stood over her for a long time. She didn't move.

His hand found the medallion in his pocket. He had to act—now! He forced himself to grasp her ankles and drag her into the woods.

At a dry ditch a few yards into the forest, Castro rolled the body into the depression. Without thinking, he threw the pistol as far as he could.

He cried out in pain. Castro had thrown the gun with the hand he'd used to strike Philby.

He was panting. His heart was pounding.

Lying on her back, Philby looked as if the makeup man had dusted her with soot and painted drying blood on her nose. "Now, relax your face muscles," he heard Cooperwasser say. "There! . . . Commence filming!"

Ever since Philby confronted him, Castro had expected to see a host of agents emerge from the woods. Where was her backup?

First, he rummaged through her clothes for any device that might be used to track her. Nothing. Next, he covered the body with branches and leaves. Hand-sized rocks he could have used to bash her head in—assure her death—were strewn about the forest floor, but he couldn't make himself do it.

Castro didn't find the hideaway before night descended. He scaled a tree with a crook between three sturdy branches that would keep him ten feet above the ground and whatever might be prowling there.

He was dead tired, but his mind wouldn't shut up.

Where was her backup?

If Philby had confirmed that Phiona Philby was with the renegade Red Cards, and if the younger sister was captured by the SSB, or even killed, what might that portend for SSB Commander Philby? Would they ever award a White Card to someone so stained? Philby had to embark on a solo mission to eliminate her sister and destroy all the evidence, including Castro Hume.

When people lose the ability to see the truth about themselves, thought Castro, *they take reckless risks because they believe they are invincible.*

The dead Philby had no trackable device on her person. Now, all he had to do was find the live Philby.

Castro slept fitfully on the heavy branches, waking for good before sunrise. Stiff, sore, and cold, it was all he could do to remain in the tree until the sky was light enough to see the ground.

He took it as a good sign that the forest wasn't crawling with SSB commandos and the heavens weren't filled with gyroplanes.

On the other side of the hill, not two hundred yards from where he'd berthed in the tree, was a low, sprawling structure, its timbers gray with age, its slate roof blanketed with moss, a house that seemed an extension of the land surrounding it.

The front door opened and a woman stepped out.

Castro ran to her.

32

Windows

All the windows in the room were covered with cardboard.

The great room featured a stone fireplace, cold and swept clean of ashes. Clement was heating parts of the lodge with propane, also powering a gas generator for electricity.

"I knew you'd come," Fiona breathed in Castro's ear.

Castro couldn't possibly connect this lovely girl with Dana Philby.

Sarah's scarf was gone, and her hair was growing in. All the anxiety and danger he'd experienced getting back here had been worthwhile to see her so much improved.

"Gray didn't know anything about this place, did he?" inquired Castro.

"No one did, except me," Clement answered upon entering the room.

Sarah spoke up. "Castro's play is causing a sensation. Sold-out performances in Detroit."

"Sold-out performances because Ron Starling's name is attached to the play and because Alfred Cooperwasser suggested he might produce and direct the photoplay," Castro countered.

Sarah finally broached the subject no one wanted to talk about. She asked Castro, "What do you know about Max and Colleen?"

He told them what had happened on the set, holding nothing back, but they had no need to hear what Philby had said about John Gray's wooden leg.

"Someone's at the door," Fiona said softly.

Fiona's words confirmed that the knocking the writer heard was real.

"You were followed?" Clement asked Castro.

"I don't see how." He had encountered no one on the way but Masters and Philby.

The knocking persisted.

"Better answer, Jeff," advised Sarah.

"Not without my gun. Sarah, Fi . . . go out the galley window."

"C'mon Fi," Sarah said, stretching her hand toward the young woman.

Castro took hold of Sarah's arm and said to Clement. "If it's the SSB, they'll have the house surrounded, and they'll shoot them down like dogs. Stay put, Sarah. And forget about the gun, Jeff."

Clement flashed Castro a dark look and walked to the door.

He grasped the handle. The knocking continued. The site manager pulled open the door.

A woman wearing jeans and a hooded jacket stumbled into the custodian's arms. When she pulled off the hood, long blonde hair spilled out.

Clement didn't bother to shut the door. "Julian," he moaned, as if he were in a trance.

For a minute, the others were frozen in place.

However, Castro's mind wasn't frozen. "Julian," the person who'd signed the letter in Clement's glove box with a "J."

Who had he expected Producer J to be? Surely, not this waif.

The custodian just stood there, looking from Julian to the open door, as if he'd witnessed a magic trick.

The woman who had masterminded the Trillium set Red

Card haven from within the SSB didn't seem like much. Her clothes were soiled, her face pale. Her eyes looked haunted.

Fiona had slipped out of the room, now returning with a glass of water and several slices of bread.

Clement addressed the group. "This is the person who made it possible for you to live on the set . . . and here."

"You did your part, Jeff." Julian took a sip of water and smiled at Fiona.

"May I sit?"

Clement helped Julian to a chair. She finished the water and took a bite of the bread.

Sarah said, "I knew someone was helping Jeff. I guessed that person had to be connected to the Bureau. I never understood why."

Julian said, "You can close the door now, Jeff."

She waited for Clement to rejoin them before answering Sarah. "A good friend of mine was desperately ill. She received a Red Card. When she most needed friends and compassion, she was cut off—by me, too. After she died, I felt terrible about how I'd ignored and avoided her. That's when I devised this ridiculous plan. I applied to the Bureau, they accepted me, and I rose through the ranks."

Sarah said, "That must have been a lonely life."

"It took me eight years to advance to where I could make a difference. I knew they'd discover me sooner or later. The Bureau has a department that hunts for internal mischief. I was bound to make a mistake, and I made more than one."

"How did you find us?" Sarah asked her.

"Dana Philby ordered me to come here with her. Does that surprise you? It certainly surprised me. Two days ago, we checked into a motel in Harrisville. Yesterday, I slept till almost noon, and when I woke up Philby was gone. Not a trace of her or our vehicle. She must have drugged me the night before because I was still sleepy and sick to my stomach. No doubt Philby figured I knew the location of this refuge, and she'd intended to make me think she had gone for good so as to follow me here.

"What Philby overlooked is I'm Bureau-trained, too. On the trip to Michigan, I saw where she stowed her pistol. I needed no more than thirty seconds to disable the ammunition clip, and Philby obliged while she was reaming out a subordinate on the phone. My crazy idea was to make a dash for it and hope I'd put enough distance between us before she could reload. I was desperate."

The reason Philby's gun had failed to fire in the forest.

Julian was still speaking. "One of Jeff's friends drove me to the edge of the national forest. We were as careful as we could be. I hiked the last ten miles. That doesn't mean Philby didn't follow me. She always has a plan."

Castro remembered the rest of what his Uncle Castro had told his mother: *Everyone has a plan until they get punched in the face.* "She didn't follow you," he promised.

Sarah took Castro from room to room. Fiona accompanied them, a step or two behind. Castro couldn't help noticing that every room had big windows so residents could view and enjoy the outdoor environment, but because all the windows were covered with cardboard, they might have been in the center of a city or on the moon.

He judged that the lodge had once offered luxury accommodations, but time and lack of maintenance had rendered it shabby.

He had told the astounded group about his encounter with Philby in the woods. Encounter was the word he'd used, and the word he summoned whenever he pondered what had happened. But the truth was, he'd killed the woman.

Almost all of the lodge walls were paneled with cedar. Natural light from the large windows had been intended to mitigate those dark walls, though what architect could have imagined this state of affairs?

The bedrooms contained only the barest of essentials, left behind by the previous owner or conveyed here in Clement's truck—for security sake a different vehicle from the green truck on the set.

"Our new home," Sarah said dispiritedly.

"At least you're safe," he observed.

Fiona put her mouth to Castro's ear as she had done earlier that day. "I take the cardboard down at night. I see things outside."

"What things?" the writer nervously asked.

"Don't worry," Fiona told him. "I only see good things."

"Let's find your kill," Clement said to Castro.

The two embarked on a clear and unseasonably warm morning, the day after Castro's and Julian's arrivals, Clement toting a rifle, field glasses, and a hand compass—electronic devices off limits here. Clement had given Castro a shovel and backpack with food, drink, and sundries.

"We were relieved to hear you survived the raid," said Clement, his voice quavering with emotion.

"How did you learn I was alive?"

"I dropped in on Masters. He helped me exchange trucks. He'd read that you and Starling were producing a play. He's the one who told me about the Detroit performance."

"That's how you knew to send me the ad for the lodge," Castro deduced.

"The ad was Sarah's work. I left the envelope at a drop in the woods close to Tawas and Masters posted it in Kentucky . . . can't be too careful. Now, answer some questions," the man said. "How many hours did you hike from Philby to reach the lodge?"

Castro shook his head. "I wasn't paying attention. I was in shock from what had happened. I remember crossing the three creeks on the landmark list before Philby assaulted me."

"And you think she was dead when you left her?"

"I thought so."

"Describe the place where you brought her down."

As if Castro had killed an animal. In Clement's mind, maybe he had.

He told the custodian about the large meadow and how Philby had confronted him on the margin between the forest and field.

"Good!" Clement responded enthusiastically. "I know that meadow. I was afraid we'd have to scour the forest. If we move smartly, we can be back by dark. I hope we find a body," he added.

Castro may have known that finding a body was the best outcome for Sarah and the rest, but he dreaded revisiting the product of his fear and wrath.

Clement set a brisk pace. If he chain-smoked all the way, it didn't slow them down or hinder their conversation. They hadn't brought overnight supplies with them, meaning the custodian intended to bunk in the lodge no matter how late. Fortunately, Clement knew this land well so that even when he took an indirect route, they made better time, and they came upon the big meadow sooner than Castro had expected.

Given the size of the field and Castro's fear and confusion when Philby had materialized out of nowhere, some time was required to identify the location of the confrontation. Clement knew that Castro had been approaching the meadow from the east. Also, the man was excellent at reading signs of passage and activity in the wild.

They found the body that Castro had hastily concealed. Before anything else, Clement carefully examined the corpse for a device that might be tracked.

The body was still intact. Nothing big had yet violated the corpse, though beetles and smaller insects were scuttling about that fleshy landscape. Was there a stench, or was that Castro's imagination?

The two took turns digging until they had excavated a grave that met Clement's approval. Though the hours till sunset were ticking off, the custodian took almost as much time concealing their handiwork as they had burying the body.

"This wouldn't get by a forensics team," Clement remarked while depositing an armful of leaves atop the grave. "But we won't give them any reason to search at this location either."

Castro had tried to avoid looking at Philby's face, but he'd been forced to do so. All the hauteur was gone, all the fear her countenance had provoked, too.

He himself had killed and buried someone, just as Kenny Marks most likely had done. While Castro understood the difference between those two acts, hadn't fear provoked both men to extreme violence? Would Marks' act forever burden him as Philby would always haunt Castro?

No sooner had they started back than Clement abruptly stopped in his tracks, and shouted, "Dammit, I locked the door and left the window open. Where's Philby's gun?"

Locard again! If Castro was bound to leave something behind, did it have to be as obvious as Philby's weapon? "Before I moved the body, I threw it into the woods."

Clement took a deep breath. "Let's find three stones about

the weight of the gun. I think I have a red marker in the pack."

Plenty of stones were about, reminding the writer of the temptation to use one on the immobile Philby. Clement inscribed a red X on each stone.

"Lead me to where you were when you threw the gun—as close as you can remember. Put yourself back in that moment. Try to repeat what you did with the gun."

Putting himself *back in that moment* was the last thing Castro wanted to do. His hand was still sore. This time, Castro steeled himself and threw the stones into the woods in the direction he remembered, each with a slightly different trajectory and force.

They found Philby's pistol within ten feet of one of Castro's tosses.

In the woods on the other side of the meadow, Clement buried the weapon as carefully as he had the body. No rain storms or animals would expose his work.

"Julian will be relieved to hear our news," Clement said.

Castro had seen how Clement looked at Julian. Also clear was that she thought of him as more than a collaborator. "Is Julian the person you had to love at a distance?"

For just an instant, Clement scowled at him. Then the man's features softened. "Is it that obvious? She's my second cousin. We lived on the same street when we were kids. But she moved away, and I did too. So, it's hopeless. And look at me. What do I have to offer?"

Castro put a hand on his companion's shoulder. "Just character . . . and who can't help admiring a man so prodigious with a fishing rod. Don't let her go without telling her. Let her decide."

"Would you care to bunk in that oak again tonight?" Clement inquired. "If not let's get moving."

Castro's shoulder still ached from sleeping against a burl in that tree. Weary as the writer was, he picked up the pace.

Sarah, Julian, and Fiona gathered around the men in the great room. Clement filled them in, concluding with, "It's unlikely they'll ever find the body."

Relief was apparent on Sarah's and Julian's faces, but not Fiona's.

Castro could hear John Gray's voice in the garden: "She's chuckin' snails. They do a lot of damage, but Fiona won't let us kill them."

"I need to talk to you," Sarah said to Castro the following morning.

"In the dining room?"

"No," she responded firmly. "Let's take a walk—"

"We shouldn't—"

"I'll meet you outside in five minutes," Sarah doggedly insisted, making for her room.

Castro waited for her beneath a majestic birch tree on the edge of the clearing.

Sarah passed him and walked a dozen steps into the woods, returning with a heart-shaped green leaf.

"Wild ginger," she announced.

Castro didn't have to ask where she'd learned this.

"Feels good to be outside again," she said, looking this way and that. "Even if we don't spot any bears or mammoths."

Her quip didn't assuage his worry. "Yesterday, Jeff and I had to go out but—"

Sarah waved a hand to still him. "That's what I want to talk about. You think of this lodge as a refuge, a haven. I see it as a prison."

After all that Clement and he had done to keep her safe?

"You say that despite what happened to John, Max, and Colleen? After what Philby intended to do to the rest of us? As long as I'm alive, I'm not going to let anything happen to you."

She smiled at him. "Think about what you're saying. For a long time, no one knew we were living on the set. Jeff had safe access to supplies in Harrisville and Tawas. We had utilities and plenty of room. The set wasn't the Ritz, but life was bearable. This place isn't, especially when we're restricted to one boarded up house."

He started to respond but she wouldn't let him. "And another thing, the business of Pedro. We should have known better, but after months of sanctuary on the set, we were lulled into thinking Jeff was infallible. I've never seen him as distraught as he was when we drove here from the set. I was sure we'd crash or flip over.

"When we arrived here, Jeff admitted he should have been more suspicious of Pedro. He hadn't wanted to admit to himself that Julian had been uncovered. So, he convinced himself all was well. We can't afford to put all our faith in Jeff or this hideaway. He's a good man—one of the best—with weaknesses like all of us . . . All of us? Fi and I are the only ones left. Gina, John, Max, Colleen . . . Ghost, all gone. How sad is that?"

"What are you suggesting we do?"

Sarah took both his hands in hers. "I'm suggesting we go to the premiere of your play in Detroit—the five of us. Draw a line in the sand. If hundreds of people see us, won't the SSB have a harder time eliminating us?"

"You don't know that."

She waited for a huge rabbit to dash in front of them before responding. "I know they'll find us here sooner than later. When they do, eliminating us will be easy—who will know? In the meantime, we don't have to broadcast our presence here, but we can open the windows and go outside now and then."

"I don't know," Castro responded.

"We're not powerless. Jeff's the most resourceful man I've ever met, Julian knows the Bureau inside and out, Fiona finds joy in everything, I came back from the dead, and you told me the SSB are afraid of celebrities like you."

"That's not exactly what I said," he protested.

Sarah looked into his eyes. "I want you to know I'm not desperate. Actually, I have more to live for now than when we were on the set. But I've been thinking about my conversation with Gina, when she told me about the law of the choice. Rather than hiding here, I want all of us to consider a different choice, a bold choice. And yes, a dangerous one."

Sarah hadn't let go of the ginger leaf.

Was this yet another moment for Castro to flip the script? "One more thing, Sarah. I want to have children with you. I want to bring Fi into our home. I want our family to be like the Stewarts' and our children to be as close as Cynthia and I were."

Her eyes widened. "That's what I want, too."

"We're as safe as possible, we've made sure Philby won't be a problem, Julian and Castro have found their way here, you're healthy for the first time in years, and you want to storm Detroit?" Clement said to Sarah. He wasn't happy.

The three women and two men were seated at the dining room table.

Sarah stared Clement down. "First, I want to tear all the cardboard from the windows."

Their alarmed protector shook his head.

Sarah told the group what she had said to Castro the day

before, how she believed that a public appearance in Detroit would make them safer rather than less safe—what Gina had said to her about choices.

"The choice to remain here with the doors barred and the windows boarded up has consequences, too."

"We have six days till opening night," Castro said. "We'd have to nail the logistics. If the SSB round us up ahead of time or en route, we're finished. They'll invent an explanation for my death, and the rest of you won't matter."

"Exactly," Clement agreed. "And getting from this lodge to Detroit, and then into the theater, won't be easy."

"You can do it, Jeff," Fiona piped up.

The scowl left the custodian's face.

"I know you can!"

The look Julian gave Clement informed Castro that Producer J felt the same as Fiona. "It's worth the risk," Julian said. "Who knows how many we'll inspire if we succeed. The Bureau's not all-powerful, or as confident as they want people to think. I've seen them from the inside—the rivalries and infighting."

"That's what Brother Gerry told us," said Sarah. "He was SSB at one time. How did he say it, Castro?"

"Their pride prevents them from seeing the truth about themselves."

Clement waved an impatient hand. "The truth also includes those dogs that killed Max and Ghost, sky hawks, all kinds of deadly weapons—that bear, probably. You suggested it was altered, Sarah."

"The bear wasn't an SSB weapon," Sarah objected.

"Then what was an altered bear doing on the set? Where did the bear and mammoths come from? You don't open a street-corner lab and produce things like that."

Julian's hand on Clement's arm quieted him. "You start

with a covert program involving scientists willing to do anything, then you convince the state to fund the program with real money, then you lean on those scientists to produce according to your agenda or lose their funding. That's the short answer."

"Professor Greenberg told me they had a deeper design," Sarah reported.

Julian shook her head. "He was either very courageous or a fool to share that information with someone outside the program. Only a small clan within the Bureau knows the full scope. It's all connected to White Cards, the acquisition and manufacture of body parts, genetic enhancement, so a ruling elite can enjoy hundreds of years of vigorous life.

"They're careful," Producer J continued. "The Bureau funds public universities for much of the theoretical research, but the applied science is conducted at top secret labs in remote locations, one of them not thirty miles from here."

Sarah balled her hands into tight fists. "The megafauna, Ghost, our big bear on the set were beta tests. The drug that remitted my cancer was White Card medicine. Then how—"

"I don't know for sure," Julian interrupted. "The Bureau's science is far advanced. Other moles like me exist, and the Bureau has outside adversaries who won't sit still while they wreak havoc."

"Ron Starling for one," Castro interjected. "He told me about a widespread confederation of talented resisters."

"After Philby neutralized me, she told me they'd eliminated Starling, then employed a Bureau actor to make people think he was still alive and had recanted his former views."

The clue Starling had inscribed on the stage play for *Seeing Red*: "writing to a deadline"—in this case, Starling's own, anticipating that the SSB would remove or eliminate him before his public appearance at the premiere.

Julian then told them what Clement had revealed to Castro on the lake, about Lucas Paine and how he'd destroyed the Bureau's tracking chips. "That's how Extraordinary Designation Card holders were able to hide on the set for so long, and how the altered bear was able to roam free."

Clement fumbled in his shirt pocket for a cigarette, lit it in a matter of seconds, and took a determined drag before coughing out a cloud of smoke.

"Jeff!" Julian cried out.

"Jeff," she said again, more softly this time. "Please do me the favor of not coughing yourself into an early grave. I have plans for you . . . for us."

Clement removed the cigarette from his mouth and put it out. "What do you think about going to Detroit, Castro?"

Leave it to Clement to hone in on the practical question. "It scares the hell out of me."

"The bear scared the hell out of you, too," Sarah retorted. "So did Philby. You're still here. Collectively, we know more about what's going on than anyone else. We have to share that knowledge."

Fiona stood up, went to the window, and tore down the cardboard.

Clement was halfway out of his chair before the expressions on the others' faces sat him down again.

A long silence ensued, until Castro said, "You're bothered and bewildered. You need a lake and a paddle."

Clement laughed at that. "If the rest of you agree," he said, "I'll do everything I can to make it happen."

"Make it happen, Jeff," said Sarah.

Castro and Clement returned late at night with astounding news.

The two men had first driven to Tawas City and purchased what the group needed to travel to Detroit.

At Evan Masters' home on Lake Huron, Clement and Castro learned that in recent days dozens of prominent women and men had published exposés of the SSB and White Cards. Several SSB leaders had renounced the Bureau and joined the rebellion. Bright spotlights were shining on Starling's rats in the basement.

When Castro checked the phone Masters had retrieved from the motel, he discovered an urgent message from Alfred Cooperwasser. The director wanted to produce and direct Castro's story; he wanted to embark on the project immediately, and he was prepared to advance fifty percent of the fee for Castro's rights and screenplay. He implored Castro to return to L.A. as soon as possible. Surely, the director knew that Castro's calls and messages were being monitored. Like those who had recently confronted the Bureau, Cooperwasser was pushing all his chips to the center of the table.

Notwithstanding the heartening news, all of them expected a raid the night Castro and Clement returned to the lodge. They huddled in their beds like rabbits in dark open country. All except Fiona, who slept soundly.

33

Seeing Red

The two men and three women who walked into the theater were scarcely noticed.

Fiona's lips framed one of her favorite words as she pointed to the last line of the cast listing: "The front of the mammoth is played by Frank Trent, the rear by Carl Egan."

Castro lost himself in the production, as he hadn't been able to do on opening night in Los Angeles, painfully aware of the flaws in his script, barely noticing the applause.

At one point in the play, Fiona leaned over and whispered in Castro's ear, "He doesn't have a wood leg like John."

As for Max, and Castro's memory of their conversation in Gray's room, he'd done his best to be faithful to Maximilian Last's request to make him "more than just a bitter slob."

Immediately after the play ended, the curtains opened and the director emerged onto the stage. "Before we present the cast, I have a special announcement. We're honored to have *Seeing Red's* co-creator and Oscar-winning screenwriter, Castro Hume, at our Detroit premiere."

Fiona stood with the applauding audience. She bowed over and over again. Clement, Julian, and Sarah sat as still as statues. Castro remembered how he'd felt when they announced his Oscar. How different this was. Not the relief he'd felt that night, surrounded by celebrities, Scarlet playing to the cameras by kissing him long and hard. Castro wasn't attired in the tuxedo he'd worn that night, either, nor would he have been able to fill it out after those five bleak years.

This time, he had Sarah's reassuring hand in his and a warmth from head to toe, no calculating thoughts or smart words to encumber the moment.

A boy in the aisle—eager and nervous as Castro had been on that long ago day when he'd met his hero—tapped him on the shoulder and handed him a playbill.

"Would you sign, Mr. Hume?"

"What's your name, kid?" asked Castro.